TO SLAY A CURSE

RAE GRAHAM

CONTENTS

To my mom, who lets me talk her ear off about things she doesn't quite understand and still has a word of encouragement at the end. Thank you for always supporting me. I love you so much.

And to all my lovely readers. May you never doubt your worth.

THE DARK

y earliest memory is of pain: a pain so searing, I wake screaming even now—a good thirteen years after. Muted chanting and the acrid smell of smoke. Waking dreams so vivid it takes a great deal of effort to recall I am no longer five.

Odd murmurings and a sharp stench startled me awake that ill-fated morning. I opened my eyes to the figure of an old man looming through a haze of vile green tendrils emanating from the hearth. The smoke stung my eyes, stole every breath from my lungs. It was the most terrible pain I had ever felt. I thought I would surely experience no worse, not as long as I lived.

But then the real pain assailed me. A searing fire burning bright behind my eyes. A dozen small daggers twisting through my brain. A high-pitched scream piercing my ears, shredding my throat, and continuing for hours. I begged for the torment to end. I swore to do anything if only it would end, pleading with all my frail might. And end it did.

In its place came the abhorrent hiss that has followed me all these years. He has been there ever since, lurking within my mind: Devoron, the monster of my madness. With eyes of fire and a body of words, though not much more than shifting smoke, he grows with every bite of his vicious maw as he feeds off my thoughts, constantly consuming my barely formed ideas. Often in my sleep, I hear his rattling whisper through my dreams, weaving them to nightmares. And even in waking, the nightmare continues.

"Good morning, Giselle!"

I glance up to see Amita cutting through the hedge with her usual bouncy gait, waving so hard she's in danger of a dislocated shoulder. A relieved smile creeps across my face as I nod in answer. The well sits directly between our homes, and we meet here each morning. Yet Ami is remarkably late today and she knows it, practically running the last few feet to make up lost time.

I can't help shaking my head as I watch her rush. I've never understood how she can be so energetic this early in the morning and still retain that energy well after the sun goes down.

"A spectacularly fine day, isn't it?" she gushes, dropping her bucket and hugging me. As she bends low to draw water, her tightly woven, raven dark braid falls within the bucket. She hurries to push it back, but it's already soaked.

"Yes, we should have perfect conditions for the party." I hand her a rag to dry her hair.

She nods her thanks and bends back down with a groan, careful not to hit her head on the low roof. She has complained more than once about the utter ridiculousness of this roof. If she had her way, we would stand under no covering at all. No matter the weather.

There is one advantage to being small, I remind myself, even if she can walk off with two buckets much heavier than I will ever manage.

"Would you like some help with that?" I ask innocently, but she must notice the slight smugness in my tone, as her resulting snort is not quite the mirthful reply I expected. "Sorry," I backtrack, then add with a shrug, "but you know I've got to get a point in when I can."

After all, she never lets me forget that nearly everyone who sees us guesses her to be older. That is, when they notice me at all. With someone like Amita around, a tiny, bland, silently skittish figure doesn't draw much attention. She always points out that she is, in fact, older, while I argue that a matter of days does not count.

Ami rolls her eyes and goes back to work, but I can tell she is perturbed. So, I latch on to the first topic I can think of.

"Have you perfected the plan for tomorrow?"

It never takes much prodding to loosen her tongue about the newest Grand Idea. In fact, it takes no prodding at all. Her eyes light up instantly.

"Well, of course." She sets her bucket down, straightening up with hands on her hips in mock severity. "How could you ask such a thing? I'm the Queen of Fantastic Parties."

"Did you just give yourself a crown?"

She thrusts her palm out as if proclaiming an edict. "I'll have no sauce from you, peasant. Or you shall see the fabled hospitality of my dungeons."

"All right, Queen of Fantastic Parties it is," I concede with a laugh. "Just don't go announcing it to the whole village. They think you're mad enough already, and I don't want to see my best friend in the stocks. What's more, your brother's birthday *is* tomorrow. Cutting it pretty close, aren't you?"

That's all it takes for her to leap from teasing to truly agitated in half a heartbeat. "Oh, don't remind me," she groans. "I was up nearly all last night planning. I hope it comes off right."

It's my turn to eye roll as she starts rambling about all the possibilities for disaster—including but not limited to: spoiled food, a twin-shaped raid, and death. I don't know why she frets so. With such a brilliant mind shining out through those dark eyes, it's rare she comes across a problem she can't fix. In fact, I don't think I've ever known one of her plans not to come off. Though, I must admit to talking her out of a few of her wilder schemes. This girl has more creative talent than half the village combined!

And my creative talent? Well...it's nonexistent. Devoron sees to that. I can't even make a conscious wish to be more like Ami. That's when the pain starts. Not terribly strong, but causing a slight spasm, nonetheless. I can already feel warmth drain from my body.

How pathetic. Only a coward will not own who he isss.

And, unfortunately, Ami has become an expert at judging between my normally pale complexion and that brought on by an attack. Still, it comforts me to know she is always watching out for me.

With this thought, the hissing in my mind intensifies.

Looking out for you? Ha! She despisesss you. You are foolish and weak. Nothing more than another trial in her life.

It's exceedingly difficult, but I push the pain to the back of my mind and ignore the voice. Ami is still talking and, for once, is too preoccupied to notice. Yet I must concentrate or she will soon.

"...which should work. Honestly, it's got me rather worried. I just don't know if I can do it this year! I mean, I have never been this late preparing before. Though, it would come along faster if you ever bothered to help me plan it." Her eyes narrow, but there is a glint of jest in them. "I don't know why you insist on me doing all the real work."

The accusation stings worse than the fire in my head. I flinch, trying to disguise it as a shrug. No, she does not know why. Though it mustn't be hard for her to see something is wrong. I've lost count of the times she's caught me in the middle of a fit brought on by nothing more than an errant thought. She sees but she doesn't understand, and I can't explain.

Or can I? I draw a preparatory breath, just as I have a thousand times before, and promptly choke on it as a white-hot dagger burns though me. My hands clench down on the handle of my bucket. I manage not to cry out, at least. Still, I can't stop the tears coming to my eyes. I can't hold him at bay much longer. And I really can't afford a fit this early in the morning.

Okay then, I won't tell her. I mustn't burden her more than I already do.

And with that simple submissive thought, the pain eases.

It feels an eternity since Ami spoke, but I know it has only been a few seconds. If I don't reply soon, she will catch on. "You are just so much better at it than I am." I finally manage a steady voice and remind myself that this isn't really a lie. "You are his sister, after all. It will mean more coming from you. And besides, you've got the twins for help. You know how much they love it."

"Yes, yes. Just what you always say. You will help me set up though, won't you?"

"I always do. That's why you keep me, isn't it? And I would like to argue that lugging the same table around for five minutes due to your indecisiveness is sufficiently hard work." This last jibe brings a smile to her lips.

My answering smile shatters as my uncle's acidic voice tears across the garden. "You wicked girl! How long does it take to draw a bucket of water? Get in here now or so help me—"

Amita rests a hand on my arm, a look of sympathetic worry masking her normally cheerful features.

"It's fine," I mutter and turn to go. "I'm coming, Uncle!"

I run as fast as I can without spilling the overfull bucket. Uncle stands right in the doorway, his massive bulk filling the space and leaving me hardly any room to get by. I hear his muttering as I squeeze past him into the kitchen.

"Useless, lazy, worthless. Why I ever bothered taking you in the Powers only know. I ought to chuck you out for proving such a burden."

Well-accustomed to such insults, I ignore him and set to my work. Light the fire, put the kettle on, make up the week's allotment of porridge. Uncle stands over me as I scrub the table and lay out his breakfast. He often watches me; I should be used to that too, but it is not often he watches me this closely. I've done something to put him in a silent rage this time. Something more than being slow at the well. I just don't know what that something is.

The silence does not last long, and when the fury bursts out, there is nowhere to hide. He brings his fist down on the table so hard the bowl tips over, leaving me with another mess to clean.

"I should think even a half-witted sow like you would have better sense than to be constantly gabbing with that witch's spawn," he growls.

Ah, so it's that again. He is a late riser and still abed at our customary meeting time. Ami's tardiness is going to cost me. Even so, my ire rises at his words. I'm about to cost myself a good deal more.

"Uncle, you oughtn't say such things. Ami's mother was not a witch." It sounds impressive...in my head. Yet in speaking, I have no hint of command, only a tiny voice barely squeezed through a tightening throat, struggling to keep the waver out. I meet his eyes just briefly with my own before dropping them to the floor, unable to withstand the fury brewing in his bloodshot eyes.

"Call me a liar, will you?" He jerks forward and takes the second bowl of porridge from my trembling hands. His voice has become deadly low and even. "Tell me what I ought and ought not do now, will you?"

"I'm sorry, Uncle!" Raising my hands in supplication,

I stumble back from his towering form. "I didn't mean any—meant no disrespect—didn't mean it. Honest! I'll be good. Never say it again. Not ever. Please."

I hate the whimper that escapes but cannot help it as I brace for the well-known impact of fists. To my surprise, Uncle only drops the bowl on the table, sloshing porridge over the rim to pool with the rest, and lumbers out the door. Most likely towards the tavern with its questionable stew and potent ale.

I sag against the table, shaking too hard to stand. It takes a few minutes to gain control of myself, but my breathing eases as I grow certain he will not return. And with the acidic voice now off to be quenched by equally acidic drink, there is nothing caging me in this hole. Nothing aside from the inescapable constraint of Devoron, leastways, but it will have to do. I fly through my chores, scarf down the now cold porridge, and race across the fields to Ami's welcoming door.

As I enter the cottage, a stray bundle of herbs crumples under my foot. Retrieving them, I take a sniff before carefully setting them on the table. These herbs are a perfect reminder of why I risk Uncle's wrath. If there is one thing I will gladly take a beating for, it is the healer who was a mother to me. And the daughter who has followed in her footsteps—my sister in spirit who greets me with a question.

"Are you ready?"

"I am. What are we doing this time?"

❦ 2 ❦

THE GRAND SURPRISE

Dusk is drawing in around us and the sparklewings are beginning to appear, hovering over the grass and dancing amidst the leaves. The cool spring breeze drifts over us, twisting our skirts about our feet and gently pulling at our shawls. It's a good thing Gil wasn't free till the evening, as it has taken the better part of both days to finish preparing—mostly because Ami kept insisting I rest.

Having a healer for a best friend can be quite troublesome. She may not know the cause of my affliction, but she can sense when I'm nearly done in, and she won't listen to my protests. However, I am proud to say that I can hold out a bit longer against the monster every time. And we still get set up on schedule. The surprise awaits the arrival of its honored guests.

Overdone for a party of four, of course, but that's Ami for you. Brightly colored pennants hang from the boughs. Lanterns light the way from the wagon trail. In the center of the glade, a small fire burns. Beside it, the decrepit table is laid out with hearty breads and dried fruit. At the place of honor sits our crowning achievement: a cake.

"It's so grand, Ami!"

"Isn't it? I saved for two months to order it from the baker. I had to bribe the twins with a promise of two slices a piece before they were contented to stay behind tonight."

"You are too lenient with them. It is little wonder they get into such dreadful scrapes." Though I know it's hard for even her father to reprimand them. Those boys are the last remnant of their mother's life. Raising the squalling babes was asking much from a girl of twelve. She hasn't done such a bad job, really.

"Well, if you were to ask them, I'm the Dark Power himself," she counters.

I laugh as a warm, giddy feeling bubbles up inside me to compete with the ever-present cold. "Then I'll tell them you are truly a genius of light, Ami." I look around at the proof of my words. "This is the best you have done yet."

She puts an arm around me. "The best we have done, you mean. Don't forget, you lugged that table around for five minutes thanks to my indecisiveness."

I shake my head. She'll never let me live that down now.

Deep laughter interrupts her teasing as two men step into the fire's glow. While I couldn't possibly look less like my best friend, these two easily pass as brothers. In fact, many who have known them their whole lives still make that mistake. Both are strapping in build, with dark hair and sun-kissed skin, but their eyes tell the difference. One has the common dark brown seen in all of Ami's family, while the other's are a remarkable pale grey, an unusual color outside the nobility.

They cease their banter a moment to stare at the luxuries displayed. "What? All this for me?" the brown-eyed man crows.

Ami laughs. "Well, you are my favorite brother, Gil."

"And you know full well this is not for you only, Gilpin," I reprimand. "Achieving twenty years of age may be cause for celebration, but for two Strikers to enter the Smith's ranks? That deserves a weeklong festival at the least."

"Don't I know it! I thought my apprenticeship was like to never end."

"You've indeed done well." Ami places a wreath of woodland flowers on his head. Apparently, giving out crowns is becoming a habit. "I reckon you'll have your own apprentices before long."

"Hear that, Gil? Now we need only find wives and we can be rich men," Eamon jokes. He glances my way and I can feel heat rising in my face. I drop my eyes just as Ami places a crown on his head and, in her typical good humor, wraps her arms about his neck.

"I am all yours then, Eamon," she exclaims dramatically. "You may speak with my father in the morning."

"Hmm," his lips press together, "tempting as that may be, I fear your tastes are far too expensive for my plan to work. Sorry, Ami." Eamon winks and turns to the food.

"And you are certain to find that flaw in your plan with any woman," Gil admonishes wisely. A two-month relationship three years ago, and now he's the superior expert on women. "Though, I wish you would take her, friend. She will not have any man in this village *or* the next."

I wrinkle my nose. Ami has told me about every one of her suitors, and there have been quite a few. One or two were a decent sort, though they wouldn't have made a good match. The rest just wanted a docile broodmare. I shake my head. And *Ami* is who they thought of? Honestly! They ought to have known she would refuse. Gil apparently does not share my view, as he spends the next five minutes expounding on the horrors of having an unattached sister.

"And men constantly badgering Father for her hand. It gets quite tiresome, you know. What's more, he can't support her forever, and I certainly won't!" You could almost believe he meant it this time, if it weren't for that slight sparkle in his eye.

"I'm happy with the family I have, and you ought to be grateful for it," Ami fires back. "You do realize if I married, you would have to do everything for yourself for once? Including your washing."

"Nonsense! I would simply come fetch you once a week to do the washing for me. And you would thank me for it, too."

"Oh, I would thank you, would I? For taking me away from a house full of work just to do your filthy washing?"

"Of course! You would feel so guilty otherwise, knowing what squalor I would be left in without you." He too winks and turns to get food.

Ami throws her hands up in defeat and grabs a slice of cake herself.

The evening passes pleasantly. We lay on the grass and talk of where the new smith shops will be. If Gil will give us lower prices. To which he strongly objects, claiming that, family or not, he must make a living. Or if Eamon will beat him for quality. To which he surprisingly acquiesces. Apparently, Eamon's skill has been noticed by several of the senior smiths. The laughter gradually dies, and I am just drifting into a lazy haze when Gil jumps up.

"If this is going to be a party, we must have some dancing!" He pulls Ami to her feet and starts a spry reel.

Eamon too rises and offers me his hand.

"But there is no music," I stall. To my chagrin, a nightingale begins to sing.

Eamon smiles and bows lower. "It seems that now there is."

Yet still, I hesitate. Why is he suddenly so keen? I freely admit it, I fancy Eamon. I always have. Yet, he has shown no interest in me through all the years of our acquaintance. I don't fault him for it. I wouldn't want me either. And had anything begun between us, Uncle would've put a stop to it faster than thought. Most likely with his fists.

Devoron would have done much worse. Erased Eamon from my memory or reduced me to a blubbering fool every time he drew near. The monster grows angry even at this small gesture. And worn down from two days of constant resistance, I'm not likely to last much longer.

Foolish, worthless girl. The boy does not mean it. He only wishes to make sport of you.

But the way Eamon is looking at me, with that intense hope not quite masked by his confused smile, he certainly looks like he means it. And as I am needed to make up the set, the best I can do is try. Just as I reach out to grasp his proffered hand, the pain reaches its fiery peak.

I will not allow such unseemly behavior!

Devoron's hissing grows to such a loud roar I can

hardly hear anything else. I yank back and drop my head into my hands. There is no pretending this time, no way to mask this pain from the others. The concern in Eamon's eyes proves that. He drops his hand to my shoulder, attempting to hold me upright as I begin to shake.

"Giselle? Giselle, be careful!"

His cry alerts Ami and Gil, who rush to my side. When Ami takes my hand, the hissing quiets and the pain dulls. It is odd how she is the only one who can do this. Often just being near her acts as a sort of tonic, an antidote. I can still feel and hear Devoron, but not as sharply. Soon enough, I find the strength to raise my head and clasp my hands in my lap.

"Giselle, what is the matter?" Eamon's voice is soft, but there is an undercurrent of tension.

It's hard to see a friend in pain—especially a pain you do not understand the cause of—and be unable to help. He has never seen me shake so. Till now, I had managed to keep my fits limited to Ami and Uncle. He must be wondering if he did something wrong, and he is undoubtedly wondering what is wrong with me. Only a madwoman falls into a fit at the offer of a dance! I manage a weak smile and let him help me to my feet.

"Nothing. Nothing's the matter. It has passed."

Ami purses her lips, appraising me. She has never seen me attacked that strongly before either. "You are still quite pale. You should rest."

16

"Oh, I'm all right now. Really."

"No, no. Sit down. And you should eat something."

All I want is to go home and recover without worried eyes watching my every move. But Ami is vigilant as only a motherly healer can be. So, I sit quietly and wait for my chance. When she relaxes enough to turn her back, I slip from the glade, effectively ending the party. At least they'll go home to happy families rather than spend the night playing nursemaid. Even Ami deserves a day off.

But they don't all go home. Within minutes, determined footsteps pound the rutted path behind me. I groan as I turn and see Eamon. Oh, why did it have to be him that followed? For Ami to see me in that state is bad enough, but for Eamon...the mortification is like to kill me.

He matches his stride to mine, placing a hand at my back without touching, but does not speak. I would give just about anything to know what he thinks of me after that horrid display. Too weak to walk myself home, clearly, and that he's duty bound to escort me. But then, he may not be wrong. My knees are wobbling a good deal.

Still, I wish he hadn't witnessed the fit. That none of them had. There is no explaining it away this time, and Ami is sure to badger me for an answer. I cast a few furtive glances Eamon's direction, but his expression is impossible to read.

As we approach my home, I fix my eyes on the half-shuttered windows. Not a gleam of light peeks through, assuring me I won't face an irate Uncle upon entry. Thank the Powers for small mercies. Forcing cheer, I turn on the stoop to bid Eamon farewell, but the words die on my lips.

He wears a sly grin. "You are looking much better."

Before I can answer, he gently takes my hand and carefully guides me in a spin. I catch my breath, but Devoron barely has time to stir before Eamon steps back.

"There. Now we've danced." His mouth twitches up into a crooked smile.

I laugh breathlessly, mind reeling, and lean against the door for balance.

He grows serious once more, brow furrowing. His hand makes for my shoulder, wavers, and adjusts course to the wall just above at the last second. His eyes search mine. I don't know what he reads in them and am frightened to ask.

Finally, he speaks. "Are you quite certain you are all right?"

My heart stutters as I realize he's not disgusted. That it wasn't pity or duty that brought him after me, but true concern. And he did want to dance, if only for friendship's sake.

I don't bother to hide my smile. In this moment, I couldn't be better. "Yes, quite certain."

"Well," he hesitates, still scrutinizing my face, then drops his gaze. "Good—good night then, Giselle," he stammers and walks out into the night.

My smile gives way to a jolly tune as I take up my knitting. One of the few pleasures I'm permitted, though I can make nothing but the most basic of patterns. Every time I attempt more, the idea falls prey to Devoron's insatiable appetite. But at the least it does not bring me pain.

I'm in the middle of Ami's favorite ditty when Uncle returns. I would not have my good mood ruined. Neither can I escape the inevitability of it—confirmed with the first roaring slurs out of his ale-drenched mouth.

"Cease that infernal racket, you insufferable girl!"

"Y-yes. Of course. I'm sorry." I rush to lay a meal. It's much too late for a proper supper, but by the look of him, he didn't bother to eat a morsel at the tavern. He'll be grateful in the morning for a few bites now.

"How was your day?" I ask, tentatively. He must have been on his feet a good deal; it would explain his foul mood and prolonged drinking.

"How do you think?" he growls, dropping into his armchair. "I whittle myself to the bone. Force myself through pain every day to provide for you. And here you sit, whiling away the time with nonsense. I'd give you a good thrashing for such ungratefulness if I had the strength left."

"It wasn't nonsense, Uncle, I was working."

He glares at me.

"Truly, I was!" I must convince him, or he'll lay into me yet. "I'm knitting you a new pair of socks. You'll like them, I'm s-sure."

I proffer the half-finished woolens as proof, which he eagerly grabs. Inspecting them with far more detail than necessary. "Well, it's about time I got some decent socks." Which is the best compliment he's ever paid my work. He tosses them to the floor and sends a hard glance my way. Raising a beefy hand, he continues, "But if I find you snuck off to see that witch again..."

"N-no. Of course not." It doesn't sound convincing even to me. Has someone told? We were so careful not to be seen.

"And not that rotten brother of hers neither. Nor one of his friends...or any man, in fact," he adds, warming to his topic. "You had better not have been with any man at all. Do you hear?"

"No, Uncle. I mean, yes, Uncle. Yes, I hear. But there wasn't any m-man."

"That's right! No man. Because I won't hear of it, do you understand?" He rises on unsteady feet, gesturing wildly with his arms.

"Yes, Uncle! Yes, I understand. Please." I inch around the table and toward my room as I speak.

"THIS is your home, and you will stay HERE!"

"Yes, I'll s-stay. Please, eat your supper."

At the mention of food, he stops short, perturbed. But his eyes light when he notices his favorite mutton dish held over from lunch. Anger dissipating, he stumbles to the table and begins ripping off hunks of bread. "That's right, you'll stay. No man would want you, anyway. A lazy wench who can't cook a decent stew to save her life!"

Then he gives his attention fully to his meal, and I make good on my escape. Blocking the door with a rickety chair, I sink onto my bed, fully clothed. I've always known it would never work with Eamon should he decide he cared for me, but tonight, I foolishly allowed myself to hope. Allowed myself to think I could ever escape this prison. Now that shred of light has been ripped from me, and it's more than I can bear. Against my will, I begin to cry.

Immediately, a bellow answers from the outer room. "I thought I told you to STOP! THAT! RACKET!"

My door bursts open, shattering the chair, and he is all fists above me. Two pains, one from without, one from within. Three voices. One pleading, one bellowing profanities, and one triumphantly hissing.

You deserve thisss. You know better than to antagonize him.

Mercifully, the world goes dark and silent.

❦ 3 ❦

SMITH'S ALLEY

I t has been a month since the night of the party and Uncle's outburst, in which time he has been twice as unpleasant as usual, beating me for the slightest of offenses. I've been staying close to home, avoiding Eamon, Gil, and even Ami as much as possible. I wait to draw water each morning till I'm certain she's gone. She can't wait for me forever, and even fearless Ami won't come banging on the door when Uncle's home. In this way, I have also avoided her demands for an explanation of my collapse. They know something is wrong, and I know they want to help, but there is nothing to be done. It's easier for all of us this way.

But today is market day, and I can't avoid going. I've been making do with what Uncle brings me for the past few weeks, but stocks are running low. My more severe injuries healed a while back and I have no excuses left. I will just have to face them.

Ami is waiting for me on the road. She doesn't even bother with pleasantries before diving in. "Out with it!"

"Out with what?"

"You know what."

"Ami, you're the healer. If you don't know the cause of my fits, how can you expect me to?"

She narrows her eyes, staring hard at me. An uncomfortable silence stretches between us. Then she sighs, links her arm through mine, and smiles. "Well, it is good to see you again, Giselle."

Guilt crushing me, I squeeze her hand. "I have missed you too."

"I must stop by the Durnin place on the way. I've never seen a new mother more in need of dreamroot tincture."

And just like that, things fall back into their normal, comfortable pattern. Passing the seamstress, Ami insists on an inspection of her wares ere we submit to the tedium of grocers and butchers. Never keen but in sore need of a new chemise, I grudgingly assent and emerge an hour later in a deep sage kirtle she thrust on me to "draw out the flecks in your eyes."

Our goods finally procured, Ami proposes a walk to Smith's Alley, claiming to have a message for her brother. I don't really want to go, and it is not only because of

Uncle, but I know she won't let me off so easily. I must see them again eventually; it might as well be now. So, I follow a few steps behind her, desperately trying to think of a story that will sufficiently explain why I have been so distant.

What if I say that I had to—

If there was a—

If Uncle—

I growl under my breath. The ideas are just out of reach, disappearing as I think them. Like a word you should know but cannot say. And then comes the inevitable searing daggers. By the time we meet the first blacksmith at his anvil, I am woozy from the pain and deafened by the hissing. I have no story to tell. I ought to know by now not to try.

We make for Gil's stall, but all the while I am searching for Eamon's. I see him just a few paces down the lane. Several men are gathered around it, presumably wishing to check on the progress of their goods. Not that they need to worry on that account. Eamon looks as if he has been wielding that hammer all through the night to meet an order. His arm shakes slightly, and his hammer comes down off the mark. Stopping for a breath, he glances up and our eyes meet. I quickly turn to greet Gilpin.

"Good morning, Gil. I see you have set up nicely."

"Hello! Are you feeling better? Ami says you have been ill for a while."

I glance at her, and she shrugs. "I was for a bit, but I'm better now. Thanks."

"Good. I tried to bring you some candied apples the other day. Thought it would cheer you up. But there was no answer."

"Oh, you could have left them on the stoop." He coughs and quickly resumes his work. I laugh. "You ate them, didn't you?"

Gil turns back to me, arms crossed over his chest in defense. "You left me no choice. I could hardly leave them for the squirrels."

I shake my head. He's the biggest squirrel in this country. "I was probably in the far garden. Uncle has had more work of late, so I've been left to manage the cottage." That, at least, is the truth.

"So, the cowardly drunk has work now." Eamon appears behind me, ever quick to speak ill of Uncle.

"Please don't."

"The man spends every evening in the tavern, Giselle." His tone is half aggravation, half pleading. "Worse, he has a violent nature that hardly needs the drink to draw it out. Even you can't deny that!" He glances at my hand, which still bears the mark of Uncle's most recent thrashing. I quickly hide it behind my back.

Sighing deeply, Eamon runs sooty hands through his sweat-mussed hair. "Harming the defenseless is the greatest cowardice I know. I just wish you could see him clearly."

Now it's my turn to sigh. "He hasn't borne his misfortune as well as some, I'll grant you that, but he doesn't mean to be cruel. His lame leg pains him constantly. Living like that...well, I know what it's like. Small wonder he lashes out at times, and then I bring it on myself."

Eamon looks in pain himself now. "Oh, Giselle. That doesn't make him right."

"And he went hard long before that," Gil puts in.

"Gilpin," Ami reprimands, aghast.

"Oh, come on! All that stuff with his family? The accident didn't help, surely, but he was at least halfway gone before."

His assertion intrigues me. I've always known something was amiss, of course. One isn't adopted by a relation never before heard of unless there was some form of falling out. Especially when one is mad themself. But Uncle doesn't like to talk about the past. This might be my chance to learn.

"What stuff with his family, Gil?"

"You don't know?" Gil's astonishment rivals Ami's the day she caught the twins attempting to paint her walls with berry juice. Then his face turns berry red, itself. "Oh, right—I guess you wouldn't." He fixes his gaze on the ground, digging his toe in the dirt and doggedly refusing to meet my eyes.

"Gil?"

It's Ami that answers. "I'm really sorry I never told you before, Giselle. Father was close friends with your family when they were young men. He couldn't believe his luck when you moved here not a year after us. But your uncle wasn't the same, and they had a bad falling out. I just didn't want to make things worse for you. But, well, I honestly don't see how things *could* get worse, now. And you do deserve to know."

"But we should give Father the honor," Gil advises. "There is a reason he made Chief Bard last year."

"Yes, that would be best," she agrees. "It's his story, after all, and I'm certainly no silver-tongue. It's nearly luncheon now anyway. Can you boys be spared?"

"I was just preparing to close when you arrived," Eamon supplies.

I snort. "You were not."

"Well, perhaps not. But I determined to right quick when I saw you. I'd be a fool to pass on that meal." There's a beat of dead silence as his eyes grow wide, realizing what he's just said. "That was not my meaning."

Gil busts out laughing. "And she secretly hoped that it was."

"I did not!" But my body lights afire, and it's not all Devoron's doing.

"Right, time to go!" Ami shoos us on our way, smacking Gil over the head as he passes. "You know better," she hisses viciously. That's the problem with Gil,

27

he tends to speak before he thinks, and you never know what will come out of his mouth next.

As our feet kick up dust, drawing me nearer and nearer to answers, my embarrassment gives way to excitement. The tale we are to hear will not be pleasant, that was made obvious by Ami's hesitancy. But it is a story of my history, my uncle, my *parents*. I know nothing of my parents. The plague took them when I was four, then Devoron took what memories I had left. But I know they loved me. For that alone, I will hear whatever I must.

Eamon taps my shoulder, startling me and drawing a sharp pang from the monster, but just the one. Oblivious to my inner turmoil, he steps to the side, indicating that I should follow. The others walk on, failing to notice our absence. I shift my weight, biting my lip. He's finally come to it, the demand for answers. He may not be as forthright as Ami, but I knew he would ask eventually. I look down and wait for him to speak. And wait. And wait.

And finally, "I wish to apologize again for my blunder. I hope it did not bring you great discomfort."

I shake my head, reassuring him.

"I'm relieved." He takes a deep breath before continuing. "Now, I don't doubt that you have been ill. You certainly looked it the last time I saw you. Neither do I doubt Carver Ackley has kept you close at hand. But I want to know why you have been avoiding me."

"You have just said it yourself. Uncle needed me at home."

"No, Giselle." His voice is kind, yet firm, refusing to let it slide. "Why have you been avoiding me?"

My stomach drops. "It's...well...I just..."

He sighs. "You are still cross with me. Aren't you?"

"Cross with you?" What is he talking about? I've just told him the jest did not upset me. What else is there?

"You're cross with me for that night, after the party. I am sorry, Giselle. I am really, truly, terribly sorry," he pleads, releasing a hectic flood of excuses so fast he hardly has time to breathe. "I don't know what I was thinking! I wasn't thinking, that's what it was—I was just so worried. You gave us quite a scare, you know, and then I was so relieved that you were all right, and you just looked like you could use some cheering up, and I didn't mean for it to—I mean it just sort of happened, but it worked. You seemed a bit happier, even laughed—but all the same, I am really awfully sorry if I hurt you, or, or I offended you or—"

While he rambles on, I run through that night in my head, trying desperately to understand what he is so upset about. We had a party. We were talking when Gil mentioned dancing. I had a fit and went home, but Eamon followed me. And then, what? Wha—oh. Our 'dance' outside my door. He thinks that I am *angry?* Over *that?* It is so absurd I start to laugh, halting his desperate explanations mid-sentence.

29

"Oh, no. Eamon, I'm not angry at you," I get out through fits of mirth.

"You're...not?" His flustered expression is adorable, but I see hurt beneath the confusion, and guilt immediately douses my laughter. He must have been worrying about this all month.

"I was surprised, taken unawares. But no, I was not cross. I thought it was rather sweet, actually. I mean, kind! It was kind of you to try and cheer me up."

"Then why have you stayed away so long? Don't tell me you couldn't get away if you truly wanted to."

I sigh and break eye contact. "I was humiliated. My collapse ended your party prematurely. It agitated everyone. And you were forced to go so far from your way to see me home. I just...couldn't face you after that."

"You were unwell! That's nothing to be ashamed of," he protests. "We were concerned, true, but we understood. You never need be self-conscious with me. Us! We are your friends. We care about you. Even," he adds with a shrewd glance at my hand again, "if it is about more than taking ill at a party."

I inspect my hand too. "Oh, right...that was an accident. I'm so clumsy." I try to laugh, but it rings hollow even to my ears. And Devoron is waking.

"This is no jest, Giselle! I am in earnest. We can help. We wish to help. But you must tell us the truth."

There's no time to form a reply, even if I could

concentrate through the ache in my head. Our absence has been noticed.

"Are you two coming or not?" Gil calls.

Eamon cocks an eyebrow and grins. "Good thing we got that misunderstanding cleared up! Now, let's go hear a story, shall we?

"Yes, let's."

A TALE OF TWO BROTHERS

The twins are sent out to play, protesting loudly, as we settle down about the hearth. The fire kindled within is unwarranted by the warm weather, but Bard Elric enjoys working with the flickering light, claiming it lends his tales a certain kind of magic. It plays now over his wizened face as he gazes into the midst of the flames. When he lifts his head, there are tears in his eyes.

"I suppose eighteen years is quite old enough to know one's heritage. But I warn you, it is a hard story. Please, just remember they were once decent men if a touch fire-hearted."

I incline my head slightly. "I knew all this before, Bard Elric. Yet I'm desperate to hear, all the same. Please, continue."

"As you will."

Elric clears his throat and begins, sinking into the traditional style. This is the tale he tells:

"Once upon a time, many a year ago now, there were two brothers born on the same day. Though the same age, one was by law the elder and set to inherit all the family's possessions, as must be the case in affairs of state. Such circumstances be often the cause of brotherly strife, but these brothers never thought of that. They were so close as to be inseparable. And in truth, the elder looked up to the younger, admiring his greater skill and strength.

"As the years passed, these brothers shared all they had. When the time drew near for them to become apprenticed, they refused any master who would not take them both. Many a master thought this notion absurd.

"'Take on two apprentices at once? Nothing good will come of it,' they declared.

"There was only one master who saw a potential for encouragement in the bond between the brothers. And so they were both apprenticed to the best woodcarver in the village.

"Now, the eldest wanted nothing more than to be like his brother. He perceived his brother's skill a gift, as their master called it, and begrudged him not his success. Rather, he set out to learn from the skill of the younger man. He watched carefully every movement made, and at night he practiced guiding his chisel just as

33

gracefully. In this way, he grew greatly in skill, though not greatly enough to match his desire.

"At long last, the apprenticeship completed, these good brothers set up shop together. They did well, and in time, each gained the heart of a lovely lady. The elder courted the daughter of a well-known seamstress. The younger was more ambitious, or perhaps only more a fool in love. He looked at Lorrella, a nobleman's daughter, and she at him.

"When the nobleman heard of this, he called the great woodcarver to him. It was agreed that Lorrella was to marry the young man only if he made a casket of great intricacy for the nobleman's treasury. Knowing his skill to be equal to the task, though just barely, the love-struck man declared that he would produce the casket on the same day a year hence. He worked harder that year than he had in all his life, living not on bread and drink, but on hope and the love he saw in the eyes of his beloved.

"The casket nearly ready, with only two days left him to complete his task, he fell ill. Refusing to be foresworn, the young man taxed himself too far and grew so weak no amount of willpower could save him from the sickbed.

"The elder man, who couldn't bear to watch his beloved brother suffer so, vowed to finish the casket in his stead. There was only one small portion left, yet it was the most important portion of all. Though less skilled, the loyal man was confident he could complete this most important feat. Had he not been watching his brother do such things for years? Had he not been exercising his own considerable skill for just as many years? Surely, he could complete one simple task to save his brother's prospects!

"In his intent to preserve the marriage, he worked with more zeal than caution called for. And so, the vital piece was damaged. 'No matter,' the dogged man thought to himself. 'It is but a slight deformation. I shall simply reform the rest to match.' Yet this second attempt too went awry, and another, and so on all through the night.

"When the haggard younger man came on the morn to collect the casket and present it to the father of his betrothed, he found only a marred skeleton of his masterpiece. Forgetting his brother's good intentions. Forgetting the dowry was not to be complete either way. Forgetting his filial bond and all they had done together. He remembered only the nobleman's edict. In his rage, he cursed his brother, vowing never to see him again.

"Late that night, there was a rap on the workshop door. There stood Lorrella. She declared she cared not what her father might say, but that she loved the young man and would rather have him than all the caskets in her father's treasury. With naught a word of farewell, the lovers fled.

"In his despair and anger at his brother's rejection,

the elder man grew bitter and thought to regain his love through force. Unable to accomplish this himself, he turned to a wizard for aid.

"Know now that this wizard was none other than Rajani. The foremost of all those who serve the Dark Power.

"The distraught man asked only for his brother to return, begging forgiveness—or, if he be dead, that just a part of him find its way back, so leaving his spirit restless. Though the spell worked, the elder brother was forced to wait many a year for the fulfillment of his wish. And when it came, it was not in the form he intended.

"Still, he did not sit idle as he waited. He worked twice as hard to make up for his brother's absence, and his business flourished. Not long after, he too gained the hand of his woman. He was happy indeed.

"Yet a day came when she discovered that he had met with Rajani. This she liked not at all, for she did not hold with the practice of the Dark Power's arts. When he attempted to deny what he had done, she saw no hope left in him. Taking with her their small child, she fled to the home of her kin far in the south, never to return.

"Shortly thereafter, the father of these brothers died. Though the elder man inherited a handsome sum, it did him no good. For try as he might, he could not buy back his happiness. His only comfort lay in the knowledge that his brother would live in want and not receive so much as a copper from him.

"And thus, the forlorn tale of two brothers draws to an end. Each did as he saw fit. Each held both suffering and yet some joy in consequence. I leave you to say which brother is the man you call Uncle."

The spell of Bard Elric's voice holds sway in the room a good while after he finishes.

Finally, Eamon speaks. "But how was the elder brother's wish fulfilled?"

"That I also leave for you to discover."

"It was a hard tale," my voice is thick with tears I can't swallow, "and I thank you for telling it."

He bows low. "It was my great pleasure, child."

Ami and Gil stay with their father, but Eamon accompanies me out. We pass the twins on the way. They had clearly been listening at the door and scamper when they see us.

As we walk, I mull over the tragedy, attempting to discern in which brother my uncle may be found, so that I may learn what kind of man my father was. The trouble is that I can see him in both brothers of the tale. And I don't think I could be proud of either.

As silent tears stream down my face, Eamon reaches for my hand. Changing his mind, he draws back, then tentatively reaches out again. I know he means to comfort me, but I can't abide his pity. Not right now.

"Just...leave me be, Eamon. Please. I'm f-fine, I promise. I only n-need to be alone for a b-bit."

Reluctantly, he bids me farewell, with a promise to see me on the morrow. He has a smithy to attend to, after all. Returning home, I have a good cry, then distract myself with all the work that must be done, and crawl exhausted into bed at nightfall. But as my eyes drift closed, my thoughts wander back. I work again to distinguish my father from my uncle amidst a haze of pain and fall asleep to the image of two men. Standing side by side. Each reaching out for me. Both calling me daughter in a chilling, gurgling rasp.

❧ 5 ❧
DO I DARE?

I wake well before my accustomed hour, too frightened to close my eyes once more and risk another troubled sleep. After a short while, I rise, wearied with this day before it has even begun. I set out an early breakfast for Uncle and hurry through my morning chores.

I can't stand to remain in this dismal place a moment longer. Grabbing a worn shawl to ward against the morning mists, I set out with no clear purpose. I could take refuge with Ami, but her home is too full of life for my present disposition. I could go down to Smith's Alley. But what good would that accomplish? Eamon won't be there at this hour and when he opens shop, I would only be a nuisance. I have nothing of import to share, after all. So, I start walking simply 'away.' Away from Uncle. Away from my friends. Away from the village.

Away from my problems—or so I hoped, but they cling to me like briars and no amount of marching loosens their hold. Yet I traipse numbly on, tormented by the memory of Bard Elric's tale, till rushing water draws my attention. Glancing up, I laugh. My feet prevailed where my mind did not. They have led me to my favorite retreat: a woodland waterfall emptying into a swift river of deepest blue. I head for a large rock nestled amidst the spray, and sigh as the refreshing drops ease my weary soul.

This riverbank is the only place where I can fully believe the Creative One is out there somewhere, and that he cares for me.

Imbecile! No one caresss about you. Least of all him.

Or rather, as I most often think, that he is out there, and it is right that he does not care. How could I expect him to when he has all this to maintain?

Yesss, there are far more important thingsss to attend to. You are not worth the time.

I rest my head on my knees and close my eyes, chanting a calming mantra. "Breathe deep. Don't think. Listen to the river. Forget all else. Breathe deep. Don't think. Listen to the river..." I don't know how long I sit halfway between sleep and waking, striving to push the tiresome thoughts from my mind and failing miserably.

A loud call startles me halfway through my final recitation. Turning abruptly, I tip into the river with a cry. The current strives to pull me under as I grope frantically for a hold, finally latching onto a callused hand. I clamber out and look up to see Eamon's amused smile, masking concern once again.

He releases me to lean casually against a tree. "You really oughtn't sit so close to the edge, you know. Lucky thing I was here."

"I like to feel the spray."

He quirks an eyebrow. "One more slip like that and you'll feel more spray than you can stomach."

I laugh. "I'll be more careful in the future."

"Good. I should hate to come too late next time."

"How did you know to come today?" I ask, settling for a seat on the grassy riverbank.

"I didn't. I looked for you at home first."

I snap my gaze to him, searching for signs of hastily cleaned blood or bruising. Uncle would not have taken kindly to that.

"Easy. I waited till Ackley had gone. When you were not to be found and Ami hadn't seen you, I thought to try here."

His words remove one fear only to replace it with another. I didn't intend to stay out so long. Uncle woke to an empty house and a cold breakfast. Now, his anger will simmer all day, and I shall pay dearly tonight.

"It was a good guess," I force a smile for Eamon's benefit, "and I'm glad you're here. But you oughtn't have come so far out of your way. You'll miss a whole day's work at this rate."

"And it will be worth it." Eamon speaks with such simple confidence, as if this is a foregone conclusion.

I shake my head. "You must go to work."

He groans, rubbing the bridge of his nose, but when he speaks, his voice is patient. "Giselle, I gave you my word to meet this morn. Why do you think that is?"

"You felt pity for my tears?"

"No, it was not pity. I don't wish to see you hurt because I...care about you. I wish to be there for you when you are upset. There are some things you ought not go through alone."

"Even if I wish to?"

"Especially then. Now, the story we heard was tragic, yes. I will even admit to being shocked. And I know it involves you deeply, but it is nearly twenty years gone. Why has it troubled you so?"

"I need to know which man was my uncle and which my father. Only I can't fathom the answer and am not pleased with either."

Both horrible, worthlesss men. Untrue. Traitorous. Ssshameful. Shameful to be a daughter of such men.

"I think I can give you an answer. But first answer me this: Why is it so important for you to know?"

A good question. Does it truly matter who did what, when the story ended so many years ago?

Yes. Of course it does.

"I think," I reply slowly, "I care so much because to

know my father will be to know myself...and I am frightened. What if the knowing changes me?"

True, true. Children are like their fathers, isn't it always said? You are the same as them. You are worthlessss. Sssshameful.

Mad.

I start to shake, though whether from the frigid water still dripping off my clothes, from Devoron's menace, or simply from nerves, even I cannot tell.

Eamon quickly moves to kneel beside me, wrapping his thin coat around my shoulders. "I do not believe it will. No matter what your father did or failed to do, you are not him. Neither are you your uncle. You are you, Giselle. Only you. No one and nothing can take that from you. Not unless you let them. But I know they have tried and not succeeded. With everything you've been through, you have never given in. Now you decide who you will be."

No, she doesn't, you idiot boy, Devoron insists with infinite glee, regardless of the fact only I can hear him. *I choose what she is! Worthlesss, miserable, DISGUSTING. That is what you are, girl. And that is what you will always be.*

Despite the shrieking hiss repeating the same creed I have heard every day since I was five, despite what I have always held as fact, Eamon speaks so earnestly I could almost believe him. He doesn't know the half of it when he speaks of what I have been through. But he is right, I have done my best to fight back the only way I know how. They have taken my mind, my life, my worth, but I never let them corrupt my heart. My heart, the one thing in my life I *can* choose.

SSSS.

The knives twist though my brain as the fire builds behind my eyes. Correction: the one thing I control only if I can withstand the pain.

"Still, it would be nice to know," I gasp out, clenching my trembling hands around fistfuls of skirt.

Eamon's eyes immediately reflect his deep confusion, bordering on panic. "Giselle? Peace, I'll tell you! I'll tell you... just, please, do try to calm down."

He awkwardly pats my back in what he must think is a soothing manner. It doesn't help. At all. In fact, it does quite the opposite, enraging Devoron. I fight to stop shaking and block out his growling taunts, his daggers, his all-consuming fire. I can't afford to collapse again now. I can't! A few agonizing minutes pass, but I mostly succeed.

Once I am breathing easily again, Eamon continues. "I believe Ackley to be the elder brother, the one who had dealings with Rajani. He is certainly vindictive enough to call on dark aid, and it explains his behavior towards you."

"But the elder brother inherited, and Uncle has no money. Nor was there any mention of the younger brother having a child, while the elder did."

"He has had many years to waste his money. A tavern

habit that pronounced does not come cheap. Though, I am certain he has more money hidden away than you know. A man as jealous as him would never leave coin in reach of others, even those of his own household.

"As for the child, who can say that the younger brother did not have one? No news came from the couple, of joy or woe. And do you not remember that the elder brother's wife took their child? Is it not possible that in all those years, the elder brother lost a child while the younger gained one? So that way Rajani's spell would be fulfilled."

At the mention of Rajani, Devoron's hissing inexplicably turns to purrs. I won't judge a gift by its packaging. I'm just grateful that with him calm, my mind clears enough to focus.

"The spell? How? Father never returned, and there is certainly no part of him buried in Uncle's garden."

"No. He did not come back while alive, nor was his grave disturbed. But children are a part of their parents. It was not a piece of the man which returned but his daughter, carrying a piece of him within her."

"And so, Uncle is harsh with me out of anger for my father."

"No. Well, perhaps in part. Yet, I don't think it's as simple as that. Ackley loved your father better than anyone and lost him. I would wager my anvil that, buried deep beneath his anger, the love is still there. He has since lost his wife and child. You are all he has left to love in the world. His only kin. He fears to lose you as well."

"You believe Uncle...loves me?" Though I am but a burden? Though I can please him in nothing? Though I mar all I touch?

"I know he does."

Eamon takes my hand, and I start in shock. He's never touched me so brazenly before. His brow furrows, attention drawn to our linked hands. I glance down to see that my sleeve has pulled up, leaving my bruise fully exposed. I draw back, but he holds me fast, rubbing his thumb gently over it.

"He may love you," a sharp edge of fury has entered his voice, "yet he mistreats you. That was more than enough reason to step in. But now, knowing he has dealings with wizards, that he's cursed kin—it's just...you cannot stay there, Giselle. You must get away!"

At these words, Devoron wakes with a vengeance. *You don't truly think you can leave, do you? You know you can't.*

"Go away?" I don't even try to hide my skepticism. "And where would I go, Eamon? Ami can't take me in."

Yes, where would you go, friendlesss girl? You have no one to run to, nowhere to hide. No way to support yourself.

"Your father he let go, you he will hunt. You'll have to go further than one cottage over or even one village. I don't know where exactly, but you must get far, far, away."

"Do you really think I have never thought of it before? If I could get away that easily, I would have gone a long time ago."

You tried once. It wasss not pleasant, wasss it? I would advise you not to attempt it again.

The pain grows excruciating and my vision blurs. I stare into a bleak haze, unable to make out the most well-known forms. "He will not let me, Eamon!" I hear myself cry.

"But don't you see?" I feel his hand press gently on my shoulder. "That is why you have to do it. He has you chained to that hovel. Terrified to stay, terrified to leave. Ashamed to even see your friends. You are not living, Giselle—you are merely existing, and you are not likely to survive it much longer."

"I'm sure I won't," I moan.

Yesss, you will. Death would be a mercy. One you are not worthy of.

"But what am I supposed to do? Run off alone to some abandoned desert?" My desperation mounts to new heights, and I actually find myself considering it.

"Alone! When did I say anything about going alone? Ami would go with you, I'm sure. The twins are old enough now to spare her. And...well...I would. I will, I mean. I will go with you—that is if...if you want me to."

This revelation shocks me so deeply that the haze momentarily clears. "Oh..."

"No, of course you don't. Foolish of me."

"What? Eamon, I didn't—"

"That's fine. It's no more than I expected—"

"I didn't mean—"

"You still must go, of course—"

"Eamon, *listen* to me!" The haze has returned, and my head is nearly bursting with daggers. I won't be coherent for long.

"Take Ami and—"

"Eamon, you fool, I WASN'T SAYING NO!" That got his attention. "Wasn't saying no...just surprised... never thought...you noticed me." I get my message out before I'm reduced to rocking back and forth, head clutched in my hands. Devoron is now so enraged he has given up his usual taunts and decided to drown out our conversation with a head-shattering, ear-bleeding screech.

And yet, by some magic, Eamon's reply reaches me. "I noticed you, love. Oh, did I ever! I thought you didn't...well, that you didn't care for me. Not in that way. And though I knew you may one day grow to, I had nothing to offer. So, I kept quiet." His shoulders slump as he continues, "I still haven't got much, mind, and the little I do have will be left behind if we run. I won't be able to give you a life as good as you deserve, Giselle, but I swear you will be safe."

"And I wouldn't mind any lack, if we were together," I grunt through clenched teeth. "But no matter how badly I may wish to, I just...can't."

"Careful, Giselle, the river!" He pulls me by the shoulders, trying to shift me further up the bank as I am in no position to move myself. "It needn't be with me if you feel you can't. I realize the impropriety of what I've asked. But you simply must leave your uncle. You deserve to live!"

And now, with my head splitting open and my body shaking uncontrollably, dangerously close to a deep, swift river, I truly contemplate for the first time what a free life would be. No more beatings. No more knives in my head or fire behind my eyes. No more memories erased or thoughts stolen. No more hissing reminding me how worthless I am. And I want that life. I want it so terribly much. And if, just *if* Eamon meant it—if it wasn't just a product of my delirium—and we did marry...someday...well, that would be a very welcome addition.

His panicked voice drifts to me from a great distance. "Giselle! What's wrong? Please, tell me what's wrong."

I feel a vague pressure against my arms, ice crawling up my legs, but they belong to that faraway world. And none of it matters now...because it is so much more complicated than he thinks. Managing to run away will not solve *this* problem. He doesn't know that Uncle isn't the only one whom I must escape...or that the other is inescapable.

But I am finally ready to try. After all, am I not

fighting harder than I ever have before? There is just one task left before I can rest.

"Ami. Need Ami. Quick!" I don't know if he understood my slurred words, or even if he heard me at all, but I am floating when I let the darkness claim me.

❧ 6 ❧

CONSTRAINING CURSE

The first thing I notice is the silence. I can't hear even a muted hiss. Nor am I in *any* pain. Perhaps I should confirm I'm still alive. Struggling to open bleary eyes, I look around. If this is the afterlife, I couldn't ask for a better one. I lie on Ami's cot, piled with every blanket her family possesses, and my two favorite people in the world are watching over me.

Sighing, I let my eyes drift and catch sight of an unfamiliar band hung at my neck. I reach for it, unable to focus until it is directly in front of my face.

"Ami," even my voice is reduced to a fatigued croak, "why am I wearing fishing net?"

"Leave it be. It will help you."

"Help with what?"

Certainly not fishing. There's hardly enough here to catch a tadpole. I examine it more closely, searching for hidden properties. Tightly woven netting, just barely enough to fill my palm, bunched in the middle around a ring of copper and hanging loosely downward. There's nothing special about it. This certainly can't be the reason I'm freer than I've been in thirteen years.

"I'll explain momentarily. First, I need to know exactly what happened."

"Eamon didn't tell you?"

"He told me what he could, but you know things neither of us do, don't you?"

"Yes." I grimace, but this is why I came.

"You needn't talk until you feel well enough," Eamon interjects rather fiercely, glaring at Ami. Though there is steel in his voice, he looks haggard. Dark circles line those bright eyes, and his hair bears the unmistakable marks of fidgeting fingers. Not surprising, considering I nearly drowned myself and the poor man had to carry me several miles through dense woodland. What's more, I must have been unconscious for quite a long time. It's grown dark enough that the candles are lit.

But Ami's nerves have been stretched just as taut. "We've been through this, Eamon," she snaps. "If I'm going to help her, I must know at once."

"What difference will it make? You did what you could. It will either work or it won't."

"There's more to it than that," she growls.

"But little you can do." He takes a step forward when Ami starts to stand. "She needs rest."

Though tempted to take his excuse, I'm duty bound to end this argument, before someone hurls an insult they can't withdraw.

"I'm feeling quite well, now. I don't mind speaking." Eamon looks ready to object. "I want to."

A tense pause of silence, then he sighs and motions me forward. I concentrate on Ami as I explain. She listens attentively. Her dark, expressive eyes never wavering from my guarded ones. Eamon's gaze pierces my heart from his spot at her shoulder. I wish he were standing nearer the door, or at the hearth, or by the window. Anywhere I wouldn't risk seeing revulsion cross his face. I don't think I could bear it.

I tell them everything—from the painful night of Devoron's arrival to the cause of my collapse at the party. Even the reason Eamon appeared on her doorstep carrying what must have looked like my corpse.

"But now...now he's just *gone!*" I search her expression for the same amazement I feel, but find it quite lacking. "Ami, what happened while I was asleep?"

"The simple answer? I put a talisman on you, which has suppressed him."

"And the difficult answer?" I press.

Her reply is cut off by the slamming door as Gil

blows in on a gale of wind. "Beastly weather. Looks like we're in for quite the storm." Then he notices me. "Giselle, you're finally awake!"

Ami intercepts as he rushes me. "It is a Constraining Curse, after all."

His elation dissolves instantly, face paling and jaw clenching. "Right...no worries, you can count on me!" And with that he turns and exits as quickly as he came.

"He's our diversion," she explains, answering my unspoken question. "You are under a Constraining Curse. It was Mother who first noticed. She was dreadfully worried for you. After the twins were born—when she knew she...didn't have much longer—she gave me the dreamsnare and asked me to look after you. So, we started making a plan, Gil and I. But I was never able to tell for certain. I didn't want to ask for fear of distressing you, and I was terrified to try such a remedy without confirmation. The side effects if misplaced can be—" She breaks off, her face darkening. "Well, let's just say it would be quite unpleasant. But today, when things grew so desperate, I thought surely it was worth the risk."

A curse? But of course! What else could explain my memory: the strange man, the chanting, the smoke, the unendurable pain. What else could explain the eternal torment of Devoron? I was too young to understand then and have spent my life thinking I was mad. Had my faculties not been so severely impaired, I would have realized long ago.

"But who would curse me?" My voice shakes. I know I was not a good child, but what did I do so wrong to earn this punishment?

Eamon seats himself on the bed, wrapping an arm around my shoulders, as if he knows his next words will crush me. "My money's on Carver Ackley. I'm dreadfully sorry, Giselle, but we know his history with Rajani. And the timing of the curse is such that I don't see who else it could be."

I stare at him, aghast, then turn to Ami, eyes begging her to refute his words. "Uncle? Uncle did this to me?"

She only nods.

Heartbreak slams into me—a riptide dragging me under ere I know it is there. The man who raised me. The man I have defended for knowing pain, for suffering affliction. *He gave me mine.* Sudden rage boils up within me. I don't know how to manage it. Yet this I do know, that traitor and I are no longer kin.

"Do not despair yet," Eamon whispers in my ear. Raising his voice, he addresses Ami. "Surely this curse can be broken."

"The Constraining Curse has but one remedy. There isn't time to explain the intricacies—and in truth, I hardly understand them. Suffice to say that victims are implanted with a soul-crushing, mind-sucking parasite. Very few live long enough to attempt escape, much less succeed. Yet, if they would try, they must take a journey through their mind. Search out the monster. And kill it."

Here she holds my gaze with fierce determination. "I will not give you false hope, Giselle. To my knowledge, only one man has ever survived the attempt. But it *can* be done."

My heart shrivels at those devastating words. Did he know? When he ordered me cursed, did he know what it would do? Did he know it could kill me? Did he ever care? My eyes prick with scalding tears I refuse to let fall. My throat constricts so severely that I cannot draw breath.

Ami hugs me close, caressing my hair as her mother used to. Eamon wraps his arms about the both of us. Neither speak a word. Simply reminding me they're there with the warmth of their love. The sweet pressure of their embrace centers me.

As I calm, I become aware of hard metal against my chest. I had forgotten my talisman in all the talk of curses and doom. Feeling out the object, I catch it up, clinging like to never let go. Here is my lifeline, my thread of hope.

"Ami," I venture, "Are you certain we must attempt to *break* the curse? Could we not find a means of living within it? This talisman must be incredibly strong. I cannot remember ever feeling better! Mightn't I just... wear it always?"

Her face falls. "Dreamsnares do hold powerful magical properties, but it will not be enough. Mother made that abundantly clear. Though I am glad it helps you. I was terrified I had performed the ritual incorrectly. Or that I had misjudged your ailment, and you should have an adverse reaction. As I said, the misplaced talisman brings dire consequences."

"But if it was such a chance to use, and will not achieve our goal now, what is its purpose?"

"The dreamsnare proper is meant to preserve dreams one wants to keep. Snaring and storing them until required for use. Yet there was once a rumor, just whispers in the night, that if one could take a dreamsnare, unbind it with the proper ritual, and hang it inversely, it could be used to withdraw a dream for good. Remove instead of retain.

"That's why Mother obtained one. She hoped it might draw out a part of the monster. That it might ease your suffering. And she was right. See these dark threads here and here?" She points to two of the longest threads near the top. "They have begun to absorb the monster, becoming saturated with his power. But it won't hold out for long. It's neither big enough nor powerful enough to fully drain a curse of this magnitude. And once it is torn, there will be little chance of suppressing the monster again."

With all this talk of talismans and rituals, curses and monsters, a terrible suspicion has been growing in my mind. Rumormongers say that Healer Aliza was a witch.

Uncle obviously believes them, and so forbids me to see my only friends. Yet I could never bring myself to think such ill of the woman who took me in. Until now. For who else would know such things?

I peer at my sister with narrowed eyes. "Ami, what exactly did your mother teach you?"

"What do you mean?"

"Well, it's hardly common practice for healers to own rare magical talismans or perform complicated rituals on them."

Her reproachful glare makes me wince. "Not all magic comes from the Dark Power, you know! Witches may be his servants, but Enchantresses belong to the Creative One. My mother was of the Ivlin Order!"

Hot shame washes over me. How could I have doubted her? But then, how was I to know there were two sorts of magic? One only hears of terrors. "I'm sorry, Ami. I meant no offense. But that's hardly common knowledge here. You ought to know."

Her shoulders slump. "Yes, I know. I'm sorry for losing my temper. It irks me still, how so many refuse our help simply for appearance sake. And to answer your question, Mother was only a Half Charm when she left her training in Ivlin to marry Father. Though I was never a novice at all, I inherited a portion of her natural talent. I make do."

"And you do it quite well. Your dreamroot tincture is

legendary. I expect I'll get to take some now? I could use a good sleep, curse or no."

My peace offering draws a smile to her lips. "There is not time to brew fresh, but I have some left from the last batch. It's not as strong as I'd like but should be sufficient for someone of your stature."

"I must go alone?" I had not expected that. Dread builds within me. My chest aching.

"Yes. Putting another to sleep would be of no use. Each person can only travel their own mind."

"I told you before, you must decide who you will be," Eamon reminds me. "That no one else can change you. If this curse is to be broken, you must be the one to do it."

"But I can't!" I cry. "I'm too small. I don't know how to fight. I'm not brave like that man who succeeded. I'll die for sure! What is the point of all this then?" A tear of desperation slowly tracks down my cheek. I can't do this. I can't be brazen like Ami. I can't be strong like Eamon.

Ami frowns, taking my hand and looking me directly in the eyes. "Giselle, dearest, I wish I had all the answers for you. I wish I could take your place and free you myself. But I don't and I can't. I do know one thing, though. You are wrong when you say that you are not brave."

My eyebrows shoot up as I regard my honest best friend, lying to me.

"I mean it, Giselle, you are braver than you think. Although, you do have a subtler brand of bravery than most. When you decide to do something, you stick it out, no matter how hard the road becomes. That is something I've always admired in you. Though you may be shy and never stand up for yourself, you possess a deep loyalty to your friends." She presses my hands so hard I hear her knuckle crack, as if she can force me to believe her through sheer willpower. And with Ami's willpower, it might just work. "That in itself is a form of bravery not many can boast of."

"I suppose," I reply, uncertain but liking the idea.

"Really, Giselle, you are stronger than you have ever let anyone see, including yourself. The way you have handled this curse for so many years proves that. Very few have lived with the curse as long as you have. Those who do become bitter and cruel. Most take their own lives in the end. But you, my dearest, you have fought. You have not relinquished your humanity nor your caring nature. And you have never given up the will to live. Words cannot express how proud I am of you!"

"Truly?"

"Truly."

Her speech gives me a gleam of hope. I still don't think I can kill an incredibly powerful curse monster in a strange mind world all on my own...but my best friend is proud of me. That counts for more than I can say.

I look to Eamon. He isn't as haggard now, though

there remains an undercurrent of worry he is failing to hide. But he still sits here, right beside me, which is a reassurance in and of itself. He smiles and takes my free hand in his. "I believe in you, Giselle. I believe you will succeed."

"And to do so," Ami continues, retrieving her tincture, "there are a few last things you must know. Pay careful attention here, Giselle! This dreamsnare has only been round your neck for little less than an hour and has already begun turning. If you cannot complete your task by the time it goes full dark, you are as good as lost. There is a sliver of chance you may still succeed, of course, but it will be infinitely more difficult.

"For, once fully saturated, the talisman tears, spilling the power out, and your monster regains full control. If this should happen whilst you are with him, you may never wake up. Do you understand?"

I nod in acknowledgment of this dire pronouncement. "I must return before the dreamsnare fills." I gulp down air and draw myself up. "I can do it, Ami."

She returns my gaze with her specific brand of fierce approval. "Yes, you can. What's more, you will.

"Now, the business of travel. Do not mistake, this is more than a mere dream. You will enter a new world—a world of the mind, but a world nonetheless. You shall need all the necessities of life you do here. Overtaxing yourself could cause permanent damage, even after you wake. So, rest when you need to and obtain assistance at every possible opportunity."

"Learn to ask for help," Eamon interjects. "Don't try to do everything yourself!"

I grimace but know he is right. Ami is always at me for trying to do things beyond me. "All right," I sigh, putting on a weary smile, "I shall *try* to make friends."

"That doesn't sound convincing," Eamon chastises.

Ami nods. "But the best we are likely to get." Satisfied that she has covered all the instructions she ought, she uncorks the jar and hands it to me. "Now, take a swig and lie back. I'll see to the rest."

The tincture tastes wonderful, the honey of lavender entwined with the musk of dreamroot. My mind becomes fuzzy and my vision drifts in and out of focus. But I can still see Ami and Eamon on either side of me, each holding one of my hands. Suddenly, I have a terrible thought: what if Uncle comes to find me? I try to ask, yet my voice sounds muffled, as if coming from far away.

"Hush now," Ami soothes. "I will look after you. You don't honestly think I would let you come to harm in my own home, do you? Gil is entertaining him at the tavern, and if the bully does come, Eamon and I will deal with him. It's high time someone did."

"It would be my deepest pleasure." Eamon looks far too eager at the prospect. I just hope he won't get himself hurt.

"Sleep now," Ami soothes. "Go to sleep." She begins humming my favorite lullaby.

The last thing my heavy eyes see as they drift closed is Ami sitting by my side, her strong, deft hands stroking my hair. And then I am falling, falling through soft, light feathers.

7

SO IT BEGINS

The feathers pass and my new surroundings gradually materialize. I am first aware of the terrible heat. I feel the sun beating down while the heady scent of scorched grass rises all about me. My vision is slow to return. Yet after several firm blinks, I manage to focus and find myself in front of an abandoned cottage, shaded from behind by a massive oak tree. It looks to have been empty for quite some time, as the stone is hardly visible through creepers twisting their way up to meet with the low-hanging branches.

I very much doubt there will be anything of use here, but with no help in sight, I can hardly afford not to have a look. After a deep fortifying breath, I begin my battle with the tangled door of vines. Finally shoving through, my stumbling feet kick up a thick cloud of dust that sends me into a terrible coughing fit. Instinctively shielding my face behind my arms, I wait for the air to clear before examining the room with little enthusiasm. The thatch of the roof has not held up well against the erosion of time. Who knows how many storms it has seen? Most of it has fallen through the roof slats and lays molding on the floor. There is a table with a broken leg in the corner under a shaded window. A few cracked jars and fabric scraps litter the floor. Otherwise, the room is completely bare. As expected, nothing for me here.

I turn to go but pause on the threshold. I may yet find water, and a broken jar is better than none at all. Carefully sifting through the debris, I find one only slightly damaged near the rim and still able to hold a good deal. Clutching my sorry prize, I hurry out and round the back, where there is indeed a well not wholly gone dry. With a sigh of relief, I settle in the shade to enjoy my tepid water.

Spirits lifting after a rest and encouraged by my small success with the jar, I eventually struggle back up and begin searching for supplies once more. There is a garden on the far side of the well, but it is quite small, strewn with stones and the rotting produce of years gone by. The only thing whole in this place is the tree. I lay my hand gently against the rough bark. It is oddly comforting that in such a desolate place abandoned and forgotten by all but the rats and spiders, this single oak struggles on, determined to provide shade even when it seems there are none left that need it.

Just like you.

My gasp is not from pain for once, but startled confusion. I have been expecting all day to hear hissing. Instead, when the voice comes, it is different altogether. A gentle woman's voice speaking kindly.

"Who are you?" I tentatively ask, not entirely sure I want to know the answer.

My name is Haldis. I suppose you won't remember, but we used to play when you were a child. You haven't been able to hear me much since he came, but I've always been there. We're survivors, you and I. Like the tree.

"Survivors. I rather like that."

Yet our survival will come to an end, and with utmost speed, if I am unable to find provisions. I was hoping to enter this world in a more hospitable locale. Instead, I am lost in the desolation with no more than the clothes on my back, a makeshift flask, and a few rotting vegetables. I had best be on my way. Perhaps there will be something better down the road.

"I might even make a friend, like Ami said," I whisper to myself.

Why, child, you already have.

I give a shrug in answer, none too sure I can trust this mysterious voice nor count it as a friend...not just yet. Though, I may not have much choice if I'm to get through this ordeal. Checking my dreamsnare quickly to find nothing has changed, I walk to the narrow, gritty road and pull up short. I have no idea which way to go. There are no road markings nor sign of habitable land any direction I turn. With a deep sigh, I give in to necessity and ask the voice, "Which way?"

Head west.

"West?"

To your right, love.

I shrug again and trudge off, hoping I won't end up carrion for the birds my first day out.

DARKNESS IS FALLING FAST AROUND ME WHEN I CREST a hill to find a large town nestled below. My legs nearly buckle with relief.

There now. Didn't I say we'd be all right?

"Yes, you did."

I hadn't believed her then, still wary of her counsel and terrified I'd made a mistake. But if two days on a deserted road with little water and only the food that could be scrounged from the rare bramble thicket have taught me anything, it's that I can trust her. She was the one that got us through, showing me which berries were safe to eat. She was the one that kept me from despair, singing songs of hope and joy. Most importantly, she has not once punished me with the fiery daggers I know so well, no matter how deep my blunder.

"Thank you, Haldis. I would not have survived without you."

I suspect you would have done just fine, if you needed to. You're a strong one.

"All the same, I'm glad you were there. Now, let's go find the inn. I'll be ever so glad of a hot supper. I may even order a bath!"

Not to be a spoilsport, but are you certain you can negotiate a stay at the inn? There are few innkeepers willing to take labor in payment.

I draw a sharp breath. Preoccupied with my lack of sustenance, I have given little thought to my lack of coin. "Perhaps not, but I may be able to arrange something with one of the other tradesmen. Even a corner in the stables is preferable to sleeping by the roadside."

I force my legs to begin moving again and reach the outskirts of town just as cold night extinguishes the final rays of sunlight. Answering candle flames peer out from the windows of a nearby home, bathing the dusty road in a warm, comforting light. A perfect place to stop. I straighten my clothing and wipe as much grime from my face as possible before venturing to knock.

A short, stout, weathered woman opens the door and greets me with a friendly, albeit startled, smile. "Goodness me! You've been on quite the journey, haven't you, lass?"

"Yes, ma'am, and I'm sorry to trouble you. I haven't got money for the inn, you see. But I'm a hard worker and more than willing to trade you a day's labor if you could put me up for the night."

"Why, you poor dear! It's no trouble at all. Do come in and rest." She ushers me through the immaculate kitchen to a stool by the hearth. "Just sit quietly and I'll get you a bath drawn up quick."

I emerge from the steaming bath in much better spirits to find supper on the table.

"There you are, love." My hostess beckons me to the best seat. "I have only a bit of flop ear stew and some bread, but it's good and hot. You'll fill right up."

"Thank you. After the berries and roots I've been scrounging, it sounds a feast. I'll see to the dishes when I'm done."

"You shall do no such thing!" She shakes her spoon in my face, reminding me strongly of Ami shooing the twins from her baking. "I'll have no trade from you, child. Don't you know that hospitality is a matter of honor?"

"Yes, but—"

"And I'll brook no more argument. Now, you eat this while it's hot, and I'll see to your room." With a vehement nod, she trots off.

Nice lady.

"Fierce lady, more like. Reminds me of Ami somehow."

Kin perhaps?

"I can't say, but the idea makes me feel a little less alone."

Well, you needn't feel alone much longer. You've got me and we'll join with others soon, I'm sure. We might even find that Ami of yours.

"No. As much as I wish it, that isn't possible. Ami made it very clear she couldn't come with me."

True, but what if she needn't come from without but within?

"I don't understand."

Haldis chuckles softly. *This is your mind, child, and she means a great deal to you. You've thought of her often enough. Wished for her often enough. I'm certain she is here. But,* she adds with a stern edge to her voice, *you won't be finding anyone till you've had a proper sleep.*

I laugh. "Agreed. I don't think I could keep to my feet if I wanted to."

Thankfully, my hostess has no objection to an early night. Returning from her preparations to find my bowl empty and me more than half asleep, she guides me to a spare room, informs me there is a fresh set of clothes for my use, and departs. I fall asleep within minutes.

When I wake, the sun has already climbed high into the sky. I rise quickly and examine the clothes mentioned last night. They are typical explorer's garb. And since explorers are men as a rule, they come with a disturbing lack of skirts. The coarse woolen trousers pair with a loose-fitting tunic ending just above the knees, both a deep earthy brown. A sturdy leather belt and a cloak to go over it all complete the outfit. No sooner have I put them on than I am longing for my dress. The clothes leave me feeling far too exposed. Still, my hostess is expecting me to wear them and I can always change later. Wrapping my old possessions into a bundle, I emerge from the room ready to leave.

"Good morning, child. I've got your breakfast laid out for you, and I'll get you some tea soon as the kettle's done."

"Which I will gratefully accept once I've helped you straighten up."

"Now what did I say about hospitality? Besides, I enjoy having company now and again. An old woman like me doesn't get much in the way of young visitors."

"Hospitality may be a matter of pride for you but being useful is one for me. So please let me help, or I won't be able to rest. Causing your guest distress isn't very hospitable, is it?"

"Oh, very well! If you feel that strongly about it, you can wash those pots over there."

Once the chores are done, I am treated to a hearty meal: sausages, bread with butter, hot cereal, and one of the freshest blueberry tarts that rival even Ami's special recipe. Far better fare than I have had in a long time, even back home. With the food consumed, we sit nursing our mugs of tea in silence. Though not with complete calm. My hostess looks hard at me but with kindly eyes, as if searching for something yet not sure what she will find. It must be good news she reads, for slowly the look of puzzled worry leaves her and she smiles warmly.

"Have a pleasant sleep, did you, love?"

"Yes, thank you. And thank you for this livery. It's... um...nice."

"Oh, you're welcome, dear! It fits you ever so well, if I do say so." She pauses to eye the bundle I've set in the corner. "You're to leave that here." Her tone brooks no argument. "Those skirts are hardly fit for rough wear. Trousers will be much more practical. Made to last and permit easy movement no matter where you find yourself. Used to belong to my own girl, you know. How she loved her adventures. She was away as often as she was home. Not that she has much need of the garb now, bless her. Passed on, you see, many years ago. Still, I couldn't bear to get rid of it, so I kept it safe to give her daughter when she came of age."

"But then, I can't take this." I jump at my last chance to keep my dress. "Won't your granddaughter miss it?"

"Oh, don't you worry 'bout that. The girl has made it quite clear she would never wear something so 'crass.' Insists she'll take her adventures in proper skirts or not at all. Leastways, it's better put to use for a good cause than left moldering in my wardrobe for the moths."

"Well, thank you again. Where is she now? Does she stay with you?"

"Sadly, no. I don't see very much of her—not that I can blame her. I'm not up to going much farther than the market myself anymore. And she lives on the other side of the river that runs through Midtown Street. Works as a barmaid at the inn there. They keep her busy enough. Why, she can hardly get away to see me once in a fortnight! It does worry me sometimes. She's such a pretty young thing, you see. About your age, I'd reckon. Tall. Taller even than the renowned palace dancer. Her hair is quite striking too, by far her best feature. Raven-dark and thick as bear fur. I did love brushing it out for her when she was small. She plaits it and piles it up on her head now, wants to keep it out of the way. But when she lets it down, she looks just like her mum!"

The longer she talks, the more familiar this barmaid becomes. Considering my conversation with Haldis last night, I can't help but ask, "What is your granddaughter's name?"

"Amita. That's her given name, though mostly it gets shortened to Ami."

Haldis was right! Ami is here and she's related to this kind old woman. Finding her shouldn't be difficult now.

My elation does not go unnoticed. "Do you know my Amita? Ah, how could you? You're a stranger. Simply passing through. But then, I have been wondering 'bout that. What young girl travels alone at night, and with nothing but the clothes on her back? There must be more to it than that. Any mystery of this sort has got Ami written all over it."

She grows quiet and gazes at me with clear, unflinching eyes. I soon grow uncomfortable, shifting noisily on my stool and keeping my eyes fixed on the table in front of me. I realize some answer must be given. She deserves no less, having been so kind to me. Yet what can I tell her that she'll believe? I decide simply to tell her the truth, or...part of it. "I'm sorry, I can't explain it all. And I doubt you would believe me if I did. But I can tell you that I do know Amita, after a fashion. I am on an adventure of my own, a quest if you will, one that may prove quite dangerous. My friends would have accompanied me if they could. It will be safer for me to go alone, in any case. As for the lack of supplies, I had to leave in rather a hurry and didn't have the time to pack a bag."

She purses her lips, scrutinizing my face. But in the end, her brow clears, and all she says is, "In that case, I'd best pack one for you."

Once the breakfast is cleared away, Ami's grandmother prepares a small leather pack loaded with enough food to last me several days, a few waterskins, and a small bag of coins. "Don't fret," she says when I protest, "it isn't much. Only enough for one night at the inn. And this I will let you earn. I need you to take a message to Ami, you know."

Before long, it is time for me to set off. Turning at

the door, I look back on my hostess. "Thank you again for all you've done. I'll never forget it."

"You're quite welcome, child! I couldn't decently have done anything else. Do be careful and try not to get into too many scrapes you can't get out of. Go see Ami. She may be able to help you with supplies or directions better than I can. Tell her that her old gran loves her and does wish she would come by more often."

"I will, and I'll tell her how glad I am that I met you." I turn to take a last look at her cozy, tidy home. It is small, yes, but sturdy and full of her vibrant life—so unlike Uncle's. Somehow, in the very short time I have been here, I have grown to care for this woman like kin. I give my hostess a parting embrace, and I don't know if I can make myself let go. I'm not likely to ever see her again. She holds me tight and strokes her hand over my hair.

"Easy there, love. These old bones aren't tough as they used to be. But you're a strong one and no mistake. Take heed, do what need's doing, and things will turn out right in the end. Now," she draws away and gives me a gentle chuck under the chin, "you best be off."

"Yes, of course. I have a message to deliver, after all." I draw a deep breath and turn my back on her for the last time. Slinging my pack over my shoulder, I set my jaw, and once again, start out down the path. It's time to find my best friend!

8

THE LANE OF SHADOWS

The sun is bright and warm on my face, giving me new heart as I pass through the cobbled streets and dust-coated alleys of this bustling town. Among the morning crowds of cottagers on their way to market, I notice more exotic persons I have only seen depicted in storybooks: traveling dwarves hawking their wares, an occasional elfin lord riding through, and even a small fairy preening in front of the glassmaker's shop. Weaving around large groups and slipping between stalls, I make fairly good progress. That is, till a shock stops me in my tracks.

Amidst all the color and bustle of a market day, my wandering glance is arrested by a distinct lack of color in a nearby lane. More than a simple bland row of houses or a shade cast by the sun, the lane itself is muted. Vague as a strong lantern barely glimpsed through a thick fog.

A fair land obscured by a great distance. The people call cheerfully to one another, their voices echoing hollowly from ages past, and seemingly take no notice of the world beyond their borders. Yet standing on the threshold betwixt past and present, gaze locked with mine, is a small child with shadowy visage but vibrant flowers twined in her flaxen hair. My breath catches in my throat, for the child is me.

Ah, yes. I believe this is our way.

"Surely you jest."

Do you still not trust me, child? She sounds amused more than angry.

"Of course, I do! You've done so much for me already. It's just..." This is unsettling, creepy, unnecessarily dangerous. I glance over my shoulder, then back at my younger self now beckoning me forward. "You know I desperately want to see Ami. Why can't we go directly to the inn?"

I promise you will see your Ami today. But there are things here you must see as well if you are to complete your quest. Don't be frightened. They can't hurt you.

I take a last look over my shoulder at the bright world and sigh. "Very well. I'll go."

The shadow child smiles and scampers into the mist. I follow with far less enthusiasm. As I pass the thick threshold, all goes deadly white. I panic, heart hammering painfully in my chest as I frantically rush forward with outstretched arms. Sight and sound return suddenly, though a slight haze still blunts edges and dulls words, and I stumble to a stop. Taking deep breaths, I search for my guide. She is waiting outside a cottage several paces down the lane. I hurry to catch up to her.

Clear, carefree laughter fills my ears and I recognize the happy child as another shadow replica of myself, not much more than four. She runs about the small lawn, chased by a strong man with dark hair. When she crawls behind the woodpile he stops and turns his back to her, scratching his head.

"Hm, now, where has my little bird gone?" A stream of giggles flows out from the girl's hiding place, but he pays it no mind. "Why, I could have sworn she came this way." Dramatically stomping round the woodpile, he begins moving it an armful at a time. "Not here...no, not under here either."

The giggles have grown to peals of laughter now. Just before her hiding place is discovered, the child's mother comes outside.

"Dinner's ready, my loves!"

"Ah, Lorrella," the man turns to her, "you must help me. Our little bird is gone."

Smiling broadly, she fists her hands on her hips. "What's this? Have you lost our treasure?"

"Ach, it wasn't my fault. She's gotten so big, she must have flown away."

"Oh, how dreadful. Well, I suppose it can't be helped. I'll just have to eat her cake myself."

"No! I'm here, I'm here," the little girl cries, bounding out and letting her father scoop her up.

"Ah, there's my little bird. Are you ready for your birthday dinner?"

The child nods her head vigorously.

"Not so fast, Rowan." Lorrella's reprimand isn't in jest this time. "Look at you two! Mud all over. And my nice woodpile scattered to the four winds. You'll not set foot inside nor have a bite to eat till you've straightened things up."

Rowan sighs and smiles down at his daughter. "See now? You've gotten me in trouble."

"I'm sorry, Papa. I'll help you clean."

She does indeed try to help, but as the logs are nearly big as her, it's Lorrella that gives the most aid. Once the lawn is set to rights and all have washed, they head inside.

I move without thinking and have nearly joined them when I come to myself. Of course, I can't go with them. I am no more real to them than they are to me, less so in fact, and my guide has silently moved further down the lane. Reluctantly, I follow, all the while looking wistfully over my shoulder at the happy family.

Yes, you lost a lot. But life can be like that again. Do not forget it.

Passing through a wall of the thick smoke, we come upon my first home with Uncle. I did not live here long and wonder what could have been important enough to warrant a place on this lane. Peeking in at the window, I see colored mist. I can barely hear the chanting of the man whose name I now know. My body reacts instinctively, much more quickly than my mind. I have already jerked back, turning away from the window, before I register what I have seen: my nightmare. My very worst memory. Why have I been brought here?

I make to run. Further down the lane, back up, I don't know which and I don't care. Just as I begin to move, a cold vise grips my arm. I tug as hard as I can, trying to escape my tormentor, but it is only my shadow-guide. For a child made more of shadow and smoke than flesh and blood, she is certainly strong. She drags me back to the window, pointing and forcing me to look again.

It's okay. This is only a memory. He can't hurt you again.

Through the tears in my eyes, I finally see what my shadow-self is pointing at. Something I have never noticed before, not the day it happened nor in all the nights of reliving my waking dream. There is another man in the room besides Uncle and Rajani: a man who stands between me and the others, between me and the hearth. The vile mist swirls about his knees, surrounding him. And then I notice he is absorbing most of the tendrils before they reach me. As the child of five lies on the cot shaking with screams, the man of thirty shakes as he bites his lip so hard the blood runs. When it is over, he turns to the cot, places his hand on the child's sweat-dampened brow as he whispers to her, and then vanishes.

My guide draws back, and I follow in a daze. Who was that strange man? Where did he come from? What on earth was he doing? And why, *why* when that terrible night is the clearest of all my memories, do I not remember him at all nor what he said? I wish I had been close enough to hear it this time.

Passing through a fog bank once more, we emerge into a crowded market square. Much like the scene I left not long ago in the sunlit streets of the town, though a cold, dim replica. But this one, I recognize; it's the Palace Courtyard back home. Healer Aliza took us once when she was summoned to register with the new Healer's Guild.

As we weave in and out of the echoing throng, my guide's eyes dart here and there, clearly in search of something specific. Suddenly, she finds it and pulls me along to a booth filled with thick, heavily embroidered shawls and colorfully beaded head coverings.

Alongside this stall stand two shadow girls. One is yet another version of myself, quite a few years older than the last, and the other a perfect image of Ami at the same age. They are whispering and giggling together, presumably about what they would do with such beauties if they were ever lucky enough to own some.

Just then, a cruel, mocking laugh rings out from behind them. They spin around to see three older, well-dressed girls with silken ribbons in their hair. The tallest of them turns to her friends.

"Aw, look at the new little dirt rags." Her remark is received with more laughter on the side of her minions. "Have you lost your way? It's easy to do, I know, befuddled by such finery. Here, I'll help you. The scullery is through that gate and three doors down on the left."

"I was actually helping the gardener locate his missing bin of fertilizer," replies shadow-Ami. "Looks like I just found it."

"Oho! A rag with a dirty mouth to match. Don't you know who I am? I could have you whipped for such insolence."

"I'd like to see you try." Indignation colors Ami's cheeks so darkly I can see it through the grey tinge of her shadow-skin. "My mother and I were called here special."

The haughty young girl advances a few paces and Ami matches her every move. All the while, my younger self has been hiding just behind her brash friend, eyes glued to the group of girls—as if she cannot help but stay and accept the doom Ami is sure to bring down on them. Once she realizes danger is imminent, however, she begins desperately searching for an out. Catching sight of someone in the crowd, her face lights and she waves. "Look, Ami! Your mother has finished with the Healers." When she gets no response, she begins gently tugging on her friend's arm. "Come on, Ami! She mustn't search for us. Come *on*."

Slowly, Ami allows herself to be pulled away.

As the scene fades, I notice the strange man again, talking with Healer Aliza. Just as the young girls draw near, he hands over a small package and walks off into the crowd. Intrigued, I strain to get a better view, but can't see clearly where he went. Standing on tip-toe produces no better results. Giving up, I reluctantly turn back to follow my shadow-guide once more.

There is less haze this time as we round a bend in the lane and emerge just outside my cottage. The closed shutters are a clear indication Uncle is home. What possible reason could there be to bring me here? Where nothing of good or import ever happens. Then I notice a small package wrapped in brown paper and tied with cord lying on the stoop. As I gaze harder at the package, I suddenly realize what must be inside and recant. Some good does happen.

On my tenth birthday, I had opened the door to find a package addressed to me. Within it I found a beautiful shawl—one similar to the shawls in the booth from the market incident several months before. I never found out who had given me such a precious gift. Uncle would never do such a thing, and of the few friends I had, none could possibly have afforded it.

Therefore, just as the door begins to open, I am startled to catch a glimpse of movement among the bushes nearby. It's not Ami. She would have given it to me herself. Besides, she was always away helping people with her mother in the mornings. I turn to get a better look at the hiding place. At first, I think it is the strange man again, but the shadow is far too small. That is all I can see before my mysterious benefactor makes good on his or her escape. I give an exasperated sigh and turn back to the happy girl just as the door closes behind her.

"Enjoy it while you can, child," I whisper, knowing she won't stay happy for long. I kept my prize a total of one day. A day filled with pain and despair, though I refused to take the shawl off. Then it was taken from me, and Uncle was not sober a moment that week. "But it will be worth it," I tell the child, "just to hold it for a day, to know someone cared. You will never forget."

My guide presses my hand, drawing my attention back to the present. For the first time, I notice bright golden light streaming through the trees several paces away. The light is so incongruous in this mist enshrouded lane, so contrary to my dark mood, that for some time I have trouble comprehending how it got there. My guide points the way, smiles, and gently shoves me towards the lane's end. It is only now that I remember why I have been on this lane at all, and where I am meant to be going.

I return her smile and nod in thanks. Though for what, I'm not entirely certain. It is clear the things she has shown me are important. But I am left with more questions than answers and no time to ask them. But perhaps, I can ask just the most pressing one.

"Who was that man? The one who came the night I was cursed. The one who spoke with Ami's mother in the market."

My guide only shakes her head and points the way again.

"Can you at least tell me what he meant to do? Was he truly helping me or only achieving his own ends?"

It is not my guide but Haldis that answers. *Yes, he was helping. You are never as alone as you think.*

I suppose that's as much answer as I'm likely to get. Sighing, I bid my shadow-self farewell. Then, I turn and hurry towards the welcoming light not far off.

❦ 9 ❦

A MERRY OLD INN

I blink as I return to the slanting sunlight and clear blue sky of the outer world. I've emerged on the far side of town and it must be nearly dinner time, judging by the shadows cast over the road. Surprising, as there is no way the trip should have taken all day. The town is not *that* large, and even my detour kept a rather direct route.

I had intended only to lunch at the inn, speak with Ami, then be on my way. I could have saved some money for necessities later. Now it's getting dark and I have yet to locate the place. I'll have no choice but to spend the night.

Turning down the alley to my right, I notice a freshly painted sign reading 'Barrels and Brands' just a few doors from the opposite end. Very odd name, but it confirms my destination is not as far off as I thought.

Convenient that the lane let out exactly where I needed to be.

I did promise.

I pause to inspect the inn before entering. It is not the nicest I have seen but a far cry from the worst. The steps are quite muddy, and a thin layer of grime covers the windowpanes, but it appears clean enough inside. I gently shove the door open and enter the snug common room, which is not crowded, but the few occupants are all men who look none too happy to see me.

A particularly beefy man rises and barks a greeting. With folded arms he introduces himself as "Brand, owner of this fine establishment," then curtly demands what I want.

I sigh. At least the sign makes more sense. But seeing Ami might be harder than I thought. Best to talk business first, put him at ease. I inquire about one night's stay and a meal to go with it. He glares but answers and leads me to a small corner room. Setting my pack against the wall, I give his inn a few compliments before asking after Ami. With a look of distaste, he assures me Amita will be up momentarily and stomps out.

"What is his problem?" I groan. "Doesn't he want business?"

Maybe he just doesn't want your business.

"Oh, thanks for that."

I sink into a plush armchair. It's not till I'm sitting still that I fully notice my exhaustion and struggle to stay awake. Ami will be in any minute with my meal. But half an hour later, I'm startled from a light doze by the presence of a roaring fire in the previously dead hearth. The aroma of a hot meal laid out on the nearby table draws me fully awake. I push myself erect.

"Giselle," Ami exclaims, turning from the dishes. "What are you doing here? And why are you wearing such vulgar clothing? That's not like you at all." She stares at me with pursed lips and a hand on her hip, as if I've greatly disappointed her and better have a very good explanation. Not quite fair considering her current employment.

"Hello, Ami." I smile weakly. "These are your mother's travel clothes, actually. Don't you recognize them?"

She stares harder and shakes her head. "I suppose they are. In my defense, Mama never wore them much when I was growing up, and I hardly looked when Gran offered them to me later. She was none too pleased when I refused. How did she manage to foist them off on you?"

"I stumbled into town quite late last night and it happened to be her door I knocked on. She took good care of me but was adamant my dress needed replacing and this would be more practical. Refusal was clearly not an option."

"Well, in that case, I can't blame you. I know how hard it can be to tell Gran no, even with all my practice. She means well, but..." Ami smiles ruefully. "Just don't let the men downstairs see you like that if you can help it. Master Brand hasn't been himself since his wife left, and we've been drawing a rough crowd of late."

"Thanks for the tip. Though I must say, I'm growing accustomed much faster than I anticipated." There's also the small problem that I have nothing else to wear. I'll take care of that later. We've got more important things to deal with right now. "You asked what I was doing here. Truth is, I need your aid."

"And you have it, no questions asked. You know that."

"I do. But I have to explain this one or you will be unable to help." I sigh and motion her to the chair opposite. "You may want to sit down, Ami. I've got quite the tale for you."

"Give me the short version, then. I was only supposed to bring up your supper. Master Brand will be looking for me soon."

"I understand."

She waits eagerly for me to begin, but I have no idea where to start. I was expecting her to know this already. Most of it, anyway. I thought it was my desperate need that conjured her here, or some such nonsense. Regardless, I was expecting my Ami. But she's different. Different home. Different family. Different life. In fact, I'm beginning to wonder how she knows me at all. I suddenly realize this Ami has no particular reason to believe me.

No time to ponder the mechanics of a world you know nothing about, Haldis offers. *The facts remain that she is here, she does know you, and she's still your best friend. Just start from the beginning, like you did before, and give her all the details. You know she doesn't scare easily.*

I take a deep breath. "Ami, what I'm about to tell you will sound completely mad, but please hear me out."

She nods her consent.

"To begin with, I'm on a journey. Well, it's not really a journey...I mean, it is...but not what is normally meant by the word. This is a journey through my mind, which is where we are now." I groan. This is going even worse than I expected. I should really practice life-altering speeches before giving them. But I soldier on. "See...you aren't the real Ami. Or not the Ami I know, at least. You are a second Ami. And this isn't the real world. It is a second world in my mind. And I'm on this journey to break a curse..."

I explain what little I know of the Constraining Curse, supplementing my poor understanding with a detailed account of the myriad ways it has affected my life. A simpler topic to grasp, though no easier to tell. At least Ami is listening and hasn't had me locked up yet. I leave out the bit about the dreamsnare darkening, though. Why make her anxious when I'm harboring enough anxiety for the both of us?

"So, it comes to this. I have to break the curse if I'm to have a life worth living, and perhaps even to live at all.

TO SLAY A CURSE

But to do so, I must kill Devoron. Trouble is, I have no notion how exactly I'm supposed to defeat him, or even where to find him, and little hope I can accomplish it either way. That's why I need you. Surely you've heard of something that can help."

She stares at me blankly for a moment, then smiles as if I've just made her wildest dreams come true. "You have come to the right place."

"You believe me?"

"I have a knack for knowing when I'm being lied to. I also know a good deal of ailments, and some curses, all thanks to my mother. While I have never heard of this particular one, it doesn't sound unreasonable. What's more, no one could invent something this strange in the moment. So yes, I believe you. As for my advice, it's the Wood of Imagining you want. Where else?"

"You'll have to elaborate. I've never heard of the Wood of Imagining before."

"Why, the wood is a matter of legend! It's rumored to be the most exquisite yet perilous place in all the Five Kingdoms. Filled with beautiful and vicious creatures found nowhere outside its borders. Men have gone mad inside, and few who step under its eaves ever return. The perfect place for a soul-sucking monster, don't you think?"

"Oh, the perfect place to be sure." There is no mistaking the irony in my voice. Just my luck. I've got to go into a spooky wood of death.

Well, what did you expect? Devoron to meet you in the town square and propose a duel?

Do be quiet, Haldis. You are not helping.

"It sounds just lovely. When can I start?" My attempt at levity falls flat.

"Cheer up." Ami squeezes my arm reassuringly, but her face glows with the cunning smile that always puts me on edge. "You'll have me there to help!"

And there it is, her next crazy scheme. One I can't let her follow though on, no matter how badly I want her with me. Fighting Devoron is one thing, and quite dangerous enough, but venturing into a wood so perilous it has become legendary? I have a feeling whatever is in there can do her much more harm than me. Not that she'll listen. I have yet to see the day I can dissuade Ami when she's set her mind this firmly. Still, I'm already fighting one losing battle. Why not two?

"You can't come, Ami. I'm the only one who can break the curse. There's no reason to put yourself in unnecessary danger."

"If it's half as dangerous as the tales say," she counters, "I can't possibly let you go alone. You'll get yourself killed before you have a chance to find the monster. And if you are the only one who can defeat him, then someone's got to make sure you stay alive to do it."

"Look, I'm not saying you can't handle yourself, just that you shouldn't risk it. I'm not from this world, so, it stands to reason nothing here can do me lasting damage.

TO SLAY A CURSE

I'll be quite safe, I'm sure. But if you come, you'll get hurt, or killed, and I'll be right back where I was before. Just minus a best friend."

She leans back in her chair, crossing her arms. "You want to talk about reason? Okay. You said yourself this isn't the real world. It's all in your head. Therefore, it stands to reason," she throws my words back at me, "my life or death is meaningless. If I do die, you will be that much closer to reaching your goal and will still have your best friend waiting for you at home. But you are real. We're in your mind. If you die, that's it, everything is gone. Me included."

Hard to argue with that. All right then, last-ditch effort. "What about your gran? Ami, she misses you. And you've got responsibilities here, you know. You can't just up and leave with me."

It's all useless.

"Gran will find out easily enough. Word travels fast in this town. And she will understand."

I notice she makes no mention of her master.

Oh, let her come! You cannot do this alone.

I admit defeat with an exasperated sigh. "I should know better than to argue with you. I always lose," I moan. "If you want to get yourself killed, go ahead. But it's on your head. I'm through trying to make you see sense."

She only smiles, gives my arm another squeeze, and hurries from the room. I finish my now cold meal and go to bed—where I lay wide-eyed, staring at the roughly carved beams and trying to find another way out of this mess. I've already paid my fee. I could leave without warning, get directions to the wood from someone else. But I know she would just follow me, and Haldis is right. I can't do this alone whether I want to or not. I don't want to, really, but if Ami comes...I just can't see it ending well. She might not be real, but she can obviously still feel. I don't want to watch her go through the pain and fear this quest is going to bring. Madcap of a girl! Any sane woman wouldn't want to come.

But she does want to come, and you can't stop her. If you fret so much over things you can't change, you'll never have peace. Courageous as you are, you need your friends, Giselle. And right now, you really need your rest.

"I wish you'd stop talking about how strong and courageous I am," I grumble. "The simple fact I'm alive doesn't make any of that true, you know."

Ignoring my complaint, Haldis begins humming a lullaby. My eyes grow heavy, my thoughts fuzzy. I find sleep at last and wake resigned to my fate. Ami is coming. I wonder how long it will take her to prepare. We will need more supplies, of course. I hope she has some coin saved up. And that surly innkeeper must be informed, which poses a whole new problem. I know his kind and highly doubt he gives his staff leave for anything less than grave illness, even with sufficient notice.

I am pondering the best way to approach him when a terrific crash startles me. The vicious cursing that follows is what sends me running. As I draw near the commotion, I notice the irate voice isn't coming from the kitchen as expected but the common room. Wonderful, an audience for the show. That's more likely to egg him on than diffuse the situation.

Barreling into the room, I see only five men in attendance. The same men who were present when I arrived and, by my guess, are close friends of the innkeeper. I'm not likely to get much help from them. Following their gaze, I find Ami sprawled in the far corner. A considerable amount of blood runs down her face and the remnants of shattered dishes lay scattered about the floor. The innkeeper stands over her, fist raised and rage simmering in his eyes. I realize with a shock that this was no accident. She must have already asked for leave. He did not take it well.

I swiftly interpose myself between them, forestalling his next blow.

Ami struggles to sit up, catching at my hand. "Don't interfere, Giselle. I can handle this."

"So can I." I gently pull my hand away. She's been my protector so many times. It's my turn now.

The man steps back slightly, turning the full weight of his hate-filled gaze on me. "This is your doing, I wager."

I hold my hands out in a gesture of peace. "Please,

sir. I don't know what you are referring to." I infuse the words with as much calm and humility as I can muster. "Whatever has gone wrong, I'm sure it was an accident and can be put to rights easily enough."

"What are you playing at?"

"Sir?"

He shoves a finger towards Ami. "The little tramp says she'll be quitting today. Taking up with a *friend*. She knows full well I don't hold with your sort." He sneers, spittle flying.

"M-my sort, sir?" Now I truly am confused. What exactly has Ami told this man?

He ignores me and continues his tirade. "I gave you room and board against my better judgement. Was that not enough? Now you aim to take away my best barmaid. Do you think I'll stand for it? Eh, you filthy little harlot!"

Ami groans behind me, more from frustration than pain, I think. "Didn't I warn you not to wear that?" she whispers under her breath.

I look down at her, eyebrow raised. "Is now really the time?"

An impressive string of curses draws my attention back to the threat in front of me. "Didn't I always say nothing good would come of letting women into the explorer's guild? The weaker sex going wherever they wish, doing whatever they wish, with whomever they wish. Well, you want to take her exploring?" The way he says it sounds more like an expletive than an occupation. "Pay me a fair price and you can have her." His snarl morphs into a leer. "Or I might just show you something better."

My stomach clenches and a shiver runs down my spine. Blows I was prepared for, but what he's implying... even Uncle never went that far, not in his worst rages. I back against the wall next to Ami, who has finally managed to stand and does her best to shield me, though she can barely keep her feet. Surely his friends won't just sit by and watch him make good on the threat.

"Oye there, Brand! That's far enough." The innkeeper redirects his glare, and I draw a shaky breath. At least one of them has some decency. "This isn't about the girls anymore, mate, and we both know it. You're letting your anger get the better of you."

"Did I ask for your opinion, Zeph? Interfere with my affairs again and I'll ban you for life."

Banned from the alehouse. That's all it takes to cow my would-be rescuer. So much for decency. The innkeeper turns back to me, fury boiling over, and lashes out with thunder-like force. As I brace for the impact, a hand grabs hold of his wrist, mere inches from my cheek.

Shocked, I turn to see who has risked expulsion for me. This time it is not Zeph nor any of his friends. In fact, the newcomer is not the kind of man you would expect to find here at all. With a tunic of fine linen and gold shining from his buttonholes, the nobleman could not be mistaken for anything less.

"Leave off, good sir. Such coarse behavior hardly becomes a gentleman." His voice is calming, though with a sense of veiled power behind his words.

Power of which Brand takes no notice. "Oh! Do I look like a highborn gentleman? I don't know what land you own, but it is not this inn. That belongs to me alone, and I will do as I see fit!"

"Sir, I warn you, I shall not hesitate to send for the constable. Furthermore, I see no reason why he should deny my demands, and I've coin enough to see them carried out. If you wish to stay in possession of this inn, you will desist."

With no options left, the irate innkeeper huffs a grudging surrender. Yanking his hand free, he retreats out the door fast as he can, swiftly followed by his friends. The nobleman watches them go warily then draws close to inspect Ami's injury. Her strength is fading fast. She'll swoon any minute and I won't be able to catch her. After asking permission, he lifts her in his arms and carries her to a small pile of bags waiting just outside the door. Beside these bags stands a young page boy holding the reigns of a regal coal-black stallion. Our savior draws out ointment and bandages from a leather bag at his saddlebow. Yet, rather than instruct his boy to see to the lowly women, he proceeds to cleanse the wound himself.

While he is distracted tending Ami, I take advantage of the chance to discreetly study him. He is a young knight, maybe a year or two older than Gilpin, and looks vaguely familiar. A preposterous idea, but one I can't shake. At first glance, he resembles the strange man who aided me the night I was cursed. Is he kin to the man? Could he tell me who the man is? Why he was there? It's possible but doesn't feel quite right. There is another explanation, I just can't put my finger on it.

He must feel my gaze, for he pauses his work to meet it and smiles. I blush, forcing myself to look elsewhere, and desperately hope I haven't given offense. But he doesn't seem to mind and turns back to Ami. Several minutes later, he informs us she is not seriously injured and will be good as new in a few days.

Before I can offer any thanks, he continues. "Forgive me if I am too forward, yet I can deny my curiosity no longer. What error was so grievous it led our Master Innkeeper to take such harsh measures?"

Ami is more than happy to oblige him. "I only asked leave to accompany Giselle in her travels. I've worked for him nearly five years now, and often as not relinquish my free day to the scullery maid. The least he could have done is give me a week or two now. But that's Master Brand for you, liable to blow at the drop of a hat these days."

"It's to be a journey, then?" He looks us over doubtfully. "Have you ordered aught for guidance and protection, or would you dare the perils of the road alone?"

"We have no firm plans yet," I inform him. "This has only come about since last night. And no matter what the innkeeper may have said, we didn't intend to run off at the break of dawn without word and only the clothes on our backs."

"Indeed. Then it seems I can hardly allow you to travel alone. In such a dire strait as this, will you accept my aid and guard, though you know me not?"

I can't say I'm thrilled by the idea. If I didn't want Ami to come, then I certainly don't want to drag a random nobleman along. But I can hardly refuse him, as he did just save us.

Ami, however, doesn't hesitate a second. "Indeed, we will. I thank you for such a generous offer!"

I can't contradict her now. "And I thank you for the aid you have lent us already. Ami would have been much worse off if left to me."

He nods gravely then turns to her. "Ami, is it?"

"I am really named Amita, though most call me just Ami. And this is Giselle, as I said before." I give a small curtsy, ready to thank him again, but Ami continues. "She is my closest friend, as you may have guessed from her ill-advised attempt to protect me in there."

"Yes, we—" I cut off, rounding on her. "Wait, what do you mean 'ill-advised'?"

She turns to me but ignores the question. "Although,

most would say you did no more than was your duty, getting me out of trouble after landing me in it." Her change in tone suggests there is some weight behind this jest.

I cross my arms. "Oh really? How is it my fault that you have no sense of timing? I could have told you announcing sudden plans to leave, and at this hour in the morning, was not likely to earn you any compliments. You have to work up to these things."

"I was in quite enough trouble before that, thank you very much! Master Brand took an immediate disliking to you."

"I know he did. What I can't figure out is why." I replay the confrontation in my head, and something finally clicks. "This is about the trousers again, isn't it?"

"Of course, it's about the trousers." She places her hands on her hips, looking for all the world like an angered nanny scolding naughty children. "I warned you not to wear the trousers!"

I throw my hands in the air. "What is your problem with trousers? Your own mother wore these very same trousers, to hear your gran tell it."

"And that shame has always followed me. They are not decent."

Just yesterday, I was thinking nearly the same thing as I dressed. I shouldn't be arguing with her over something so trivial. Yet being unjustly accused goads me on. "They are practical," I reply stiffly. "And quite comfortable, I might add." Her quip about shame finally registers, and I grow truly angry. "How dare you talk about your mother like that! She was a wonderful woman. If trousers were good enough for her, then they are good enough for me." This last jab is accompanied by a firm shake of my head. I never thought I would feel so strongly about clothing.

"They give the wrong impression!" Ami is all but screaming in my face now. "Even mother admitted that in the end. Didn't I tell you she had stopped wearing them by the time I was born? You heard what Brand said, and it's not the first time I've been called such. Through no fault of my own, I might add. Men will think what they like, but you needn't encourage them to it!"

This gives me pause. I knew I could get myself in trouble but hadn't thought how it would reflect on her. "Fine, I'm sorry." My apology is less than graceful, but I'm not in a very generous mood. "I'm sorry about the trousers, but this is all I've got. Are you happy now?" My outburst shocks her mute. Not an easy thing to do. I try hard to swallow down my anger, but Ami's glaring doesn't help.

After a minute or so, the page boy giggles nervously, breaking the seething silence and reminding us we are not alone. He is swiftly hushed, but Ami turns beet red, and I'm too mortified to speak. Our eyes meet, and I can see the apology written there; no need to voice it. I slowly face the men as Ami starts to apologize to them as well.

She has hardly begun when the nobleman interrupts her, hands raised. "Peace, there is nothing to forgive. You have been abominably misused. Your anger is justified."

"But not my actions. Please, sir, accept my apology."

Our savior nods into silence again. A beat later he clears his throat and forces a more cheerful air. "Well then, Lady Ami, Lady Giselle." He gives a half-bow to each of us. "As you have given me your names, I had better give you mine. I am Elden. My boy here is called Leal. Pleased to make your acquaintance. And now, where is it you are bound?"

"We have a sort of...well, I suppose you could call it a quest. There's something I must track down, and we believe it can be found in the Wood of Imagining."

The boy's eyes light up with an excitement usually reserved for the Feast of Gifts. "A quest! Oh, I've always wanted to go on a proper quest, my lord. Can we? Please?"

"I know that all too well, Leal," his master reprimands with a short sigh. "But to *that* wood? Is there no other way to obtain this thing you seek? Do you not know what perils lie within?"

"I suppose we do, sir. Or at least, Ami has heard the tales. All I know is this will not be much of a holiday. But we truly have no other choice."

You need to explain it properly. If you want his help, he needs to know.

Reluctant to explain everything yet again, and to someone I trust far less, I give him a cursory overview. Little more than the fact I must kill a monster and fully omitting the other world bits. Don't want him to think I'm *completely* mad. "Are you still willing to accompany us?" I ask once he is aware of what he has gotten himself into.

"Why, now more than ever, my good lady. Let it not be said Lord Elden Richardson ever went back on his word! Certainly not out of fear. Nor could I in good conscience permit two maidens, strong as they be, to undertake such a quest unaided. Now, you said your provisions had yet to be gathered. Go and do so. Meanwhile, I shall attend the market and obtain any necessary items you may miss. We convene here at the turning of the hour."

❦ 10 ❦

UNDER LEAF AND BOUGH

I spot it on the horizon when we break for a late luncheon the next day. The Wood of Imagining. It appears innocuous from here, just your common mixed-leaf wood. Hardly worth its grim reputation. Yet Ami is adamant that few explorers who enter its bounds return alive, while those who do bring with them a trove of tales. Tales of lurking power and lethal predators, of monsters and madness, of woe and betrayal. All which she has relished sharing.

Nightfall finds us upon the very edge of the wood. It's a good deal more menacing now, looming out of the gloom, and I have no problem believing the tales. A vast curving green wall spread tall and thick in front of us. Every now and then an eerie, moaning howl echoes out from among the twisting branches. I try not to dwell on them, thankful for one more night before I must muster up enough courage to go in.

Elden gathers fallen branches for a fire, careful not to stray far inside or take directly from the trees. "Break no limbs unless you must whilst we remain in the wood," he warns us. "I have heard some of these trees bear fierce guardians. Though I know not which, I am unwilling to take the risk."

Rather than risk it myself, I help Leal with Shadegleam. That's my name for the stallion. One I thought of when I noticed the bright star on his forehead, gleaming amidst the nightshade of his coat. I'm quite partial to it, and so have not ventured to seek Lord Elden's approval in fear it may be denied. I've never gotten to name anything before, and this brings me a sort of pride. It came as quite the pleasant shock when the word sprang to mind without so much as a twinge of pain. A circumstance of which I aim to take full advantage.

I stroke between his twitching ears, hoping to calm him from the wood's dark influence. He nickers, nudging his velvet nose against my hand. If only I could so readily be put at ease. Sighing, I drag myself away and begin laying out supplies.

"Here, let me take that." Ami reaches for the pack I have just unlashed.

I hesitate. The bag isn't all that heavy. She could normally handle it without a problem, much easier than

I in fact, but I'm not sure she should try so recently after a head injury.

"No, I can do it. Besides, Leal is enough help for two. Go sit down."

She has exerted herself far too much already these past two days. We let her ride as often as possible, but we couldn't overburden the horse and the road has taken its toll.

"Here, Lady Ami, I have made a cushion up for you." Leal gestures to a seat that will soon be nearest the fire. Ami smiles at him but doesn't move. "Please do sit, my lady. Head wounds are dangerous. Trust me, I've seen many!" He says it with a tinge of both pride and disgust in his voice.

"Powers save me from you two." She crosses her arms. "I know my own fair share about wounds, thank you very much. I bear a mere scratch and am hardly an invalid! If I could march all day, I can help you make camp now."

"No, Ami. Rest."

Though not life-threatening, the injury is certainly more than a scratch. Even Lord Elden said it would take several days to heal properly.

"Giselle—"

"Sit. Now." Ironic, how our roles have reversed in so short a time.

She glowers. But when I don't back down and Leal asks again, she throws her hands up with a huff and stomps over to the cushion. No sooner has she sat than the eager boy thrusts an extra blanket upon her. I laugh as I watch her ire mount. It feels good to be in charge for once.

By the time Elden has gathered a suitable amount of wood, we have everything set to rights. Soon a cheerful blaze glows, over which a hearty supper bubbles. A few tales are told before sleep, most of them by an overexcited Leal. As I try to keep track with his convoluted story about a feral badger he apparently fought to the death, my glance flits over Lord Elden. That pounding, puzzled feeling wraps around my head once again. Is this the first time we have met? I honestly don't think so. Though I can't recall any certain instance of having seen him before. Nor has he shown any familiarity towards me. Add to this the fact that he is a nobleman, or the fact that I have never known anyone named Elden for that matter, and it is not possible that we know each other. But there is just something about him that draws me in.

Of course, it may be nothing more than the charisma of a leader and my gratefulness for his help. As I slowly drift between the land of waking and that of dreamers, I become aware of a soft tinkling, accompanied by slight flashes of light in the grass. Like there are many small mirrors hidden over the ground, reflecting the firelight. Strange. But I am too tired to investigate.

I WAKE TO THE SAME ODD TINKLING THAT LULLED ME asleep. As I roll over, I catch sight of movement in the grass and lie still as stone. Peering closely at a spot just to the right of my pack, I spy a creature reminiscent of a spider—yet unlike any spider I have ever laid eyes on. It's large as a man's fist and roughly in the shape of an inkwell. Though it has eight legs, they sit not in neat rows but two on each of its four sides. And it has but two small eyes, placed directly in the front. Most intriguing, however, is its hide: translucent as glass and holding a deep black substance within.

I call the others to see, but it scuttles off much faster than I anticipated. My attempts to describe this 'inkwell spider' are met with confused stares, and I conclude it is not a common creature. It must have come from somewhere within the wood, called out by the warmth and noise of our fire. This gives me hope, for I did not find it alarming and perhaps not everything we will meet under those dark leaves will be vicious monsters.

Though Ami is less inclined to agree, I set out this morning with a lighter heart than I've had in a long time. Unfortunately, my good mood persists but an hour under the trees. The further in we go, the more difficult the trek becomes. Dense underbrush and a tangle of briars catch at my every step. The air grows thick and stale, so that drawing breath becomes a chore. It does not take me long to realize how grateful I am for my proper explorer's clothing, even if it did get me in trouble. Watching Ami struggle to make it through the muck in a skirt tells me I could never have managed it. The day wears slowly down in endless toil, and there is not even a path to follow.

Did you expect one? When so few set foot under this canopy of leaves?

It seems I've amused Haldis again. At least one of us is enjoying themselves.

You are forging your own path now. That's what they do in all the great tales.

"Well, those great tales never make it sound this unpleasant," I mutter under my breath.

Pleasant things are often not worth much without the unpleasantness it takes to get at them.

Oh, shut up.

Even worse than the pathless maze, however, is the green dusk. The trees grow up so tall and close together that one can hardly see for lack of proper light. The only indication of time passing is the void morphing from green to grey and the reappearance of the inky creatures around our campfire each evening. They are an oddly inquisitive, friendly bunch, scurrying their way over bags and up shoulders to inspect whatever catches their fancy with a happy little tinkling. Leal takes great delight in trying to teach them tricks, and even Ami grudgingly accepts them as part of the daily routine.

Nearly a week passes in this bewildering way. Ami's head wound heals nicely, but by the end of the second day, her skirts are in such bad state that Lord Elden is forced to lend her a spare pair of his trousers. She grumbles at first, but pipes down when she realizes just how easy it is to walk. The result of her free movement, naturally, is that she grows overeager and tries to scout ahead while we rest. When we finally catch up to her, she is cornered by a shimmering boar-like creature, which Lord Elden swiftly dispatches.

Both a blessing and a curse, the boar provides us with more meat than we can possibly eat before it spoils, while convincing Lord Elden that even peasant women ought to learn at least the rudiments of fighting. When we make camp that night, he disappears for a while and returns with several long staves. I don't ask how he got them without damaging any trees, but judging by the state of his disheveled appearance, I'm sure it was not pleasant. After dinner he sets to work whittling the ends to points and hardening them in the fire, producing rather crude but passable spears.

So, thanks to Ami's trousers, we now must trudge all day and take a beating every evening. Though I must admit I am sure to need these skills in time, I'm not convinced any amount of training will do me much good. Ami has always been naturally graceful, and Lord Elden highly praises her skill for adaptation each night he pairs with her. I, on the other hand, have yet to make a fair match for Leal, who can't have been through much more training than myself at his age.

Apart from soundly trouncing me in practice, the boy has taken it upon himself to provide us entertainment. I'm beginning to think he should be training as a bard rather than a knight. His mouth runs like a river, coursing down song after tale after song, whether we will it or not. Though, he does complain now and then; at which point, he is curtly reminded that he wanted to go on a quest and told to keep quiet. But the suffocating lack of clean air and light is wearing on all of us.

While our trials are producing sluggish results in combat training, I can't see that we are making any progress through the wood. We might as well be walking in place the whole day long. Meanwhile, my dreamsnare is progressing at an alarming rate. I have taken to checking it obsessively, as there isn't much else to do, and I'm beginning to worry we will accomplish nothing at all before the time is up. At first, it was hard to see the difference from one day to the next. But the pace has significantly increased over the last two and my nerves are drawn taut.

However, this evening we finally strike upon a bit of luck. Heat sick and sorer than I have ever been in my life, we stumble into a small dell. The first such place we have come across. There is a large tree standing in the middle, but the rest is blessedly open to the sky. I drop down to stretch out in the waning sunlight, desperately hoping training might be put off, just for tonight. A cool, fresh breeze kicks up to ruffle our hair and play among the grasses. I close my eyes with a sigh, quite content to lay here and drift into unconsciousness.

"My lord, I think we ought not stay here," Leal whispers.

"Come now, Leal," Lord Elden groans. "Don't be so difficult. What could you possibly object to? Is this not pleasant?"

"True, my lord. But a bit too pleasant, I'd say. Look how the clearing is perfectly round. And this tree stands directly in the center. It isn't natural."

Stay alert! The boy makes a good observation.

I pry my eyes open with the sinking suspicion they are right. But I refuse to admit it aloud. I just cannot make myself walk any longer. Thankfully, it isn't my place to become involved in a nobleman's debate with his page.

"My boy, you see danger in the simplest of things!" He declares it with confidence but shuffles his feet as if just as uncomfortable with the situation. "Be thankful! We have found a pleasant campsite, and I won't require the ladies to struggle on in the thick again tonight." He may say it's for my and Ami's benefit, but no doubt he needs the rest most. He has made sure to walk in the front since we entered the wood, cutting a path through the brush.

"But, my lord..."

"Leal, I will not say it again. Hold your tongue and make camp."

The boy grumbles but does as he's told. I force myself up to help Ami prepare a hasty meal, though we light no fire—Lord Elden's one concession to Leal's fretting. When I finally climb into my bedroll, I have just enough coherence left to notice the spiders have not shown tonight and wonder if it's the ill feel of our resting place or only the lack of warmth that keeps them away.

I'm vaguely aware of poor Leal fidgeting beside me. Too anxious to sleep, he eventually decides to sit up with his bow in hand. There's a part of me that feels I ought to keep watch with him, but my eyes are heavy as lead and I can't fight them any longer. My rest is fitful, disturbed by dreams of glowing eyes watching us from the tree line. But nothing draws me from my slumber till the grey dusk before dawn.

A CURIOUS SENSATION WAKES ME—THE SAME TINGLING down my back that I often feel when strangers watch me pass by in the marketplace. Rising quickly, I scan the dell. Leal still sits propped against the tree, but it seems his vigil grew too much for him and he nodded off. Seeing nothing else, I try to put it out of my mind and wake the others. Leal jumps straight up. He takes one glance around and immediately begins packing. The others are not so eager. It takes several minutes for me to shake Ami awake, and I don't even attempt Lord Elden. Leal can deal with that. But getting them up was only half the battle.

"I know it's still early and the sun has not yet risen," I start, "but there is just enough light to see by. I think we should be getting on."

"Why?" asks Ami. "What's happened?"

"Nothing. At least, not yet. But I have this queer feeling, like someone is watching me, like the trees are spying on us. I dreamt of it, too. I don't think I'll be easy until we are on the move again."

Shadegleam whinnies as if in agreement. Though a strong warhorse, the dell seems to frighten him. He is skittish, ears swiveling this way and that, as if searching for something. Leal, face white as a sheet, tries to hold him still without much success. He doesn't say anything, but it is obvious he still thinks the place cursed and wants to leave.

After a moments silence, Elden acquiesces. "Very well. Now that I have rested, I cannot in truth say I feel quite at ease here either," he admits. "Let us break camp as quickly as may be. We can take a walking breakfast if needs must."

The eternal question of which way we ought to go, however, presents a delay. Ami and Elden discuss the predicament as they have every morning, debating which direction we are most likely to find a water source. We have kept our food stocks well supplemented with the abundance of small game, but our water is running dangerously low. No one expected it would take this long to come across a river. Even a small stream would do.

But more importantly, we have no idea in which direction our quest's goal lies. My dreamsnare grows darker by the day, the hour even. Not that they know. But I've made it clear we must locate Devoron, and soon.

"From the tales I have heard, a creature of this sort would prefer hard terrain, more desolate, empty," Elden states.

"Desolate and empty? Really?" Ami has a slight edge of hysteria to her voice as she twists her hair. "We are in the middle of a forest! It can hardly get less empty."

"True. So where might we find a rocky area in a forest this size?"

"We won't. And we ought to be concentrating on the water supply first. We will never find the monster if we die of thirst."

"All the water in the forest will be of no use if we hold course in the wrong direction."

They go back and forth, not reaching any decision and wearing down everyone's already thin patience. Leal stands quietly stroking the horse. I almost wonder if his fright has left him mute. I have never known him to hold his tongue this long.

As they argue, a chill runs over me. I'm more certain than ever we are being watched. But my search reveals only winking lights far off. Leal is frantically scanning the ridge too, trying to turn without being trod on by Shadegleam, who is becoming more agitated by the moment. His ears have stopped swiveling to lay straight back on his head. His nostrils flare and he paws the ground with his right foreleg. Perhaps he can see the danger we cannot.

Look! Over there on the left.

I turn at Haldis' command and just catch sight of movement on the edge of the tree line. A dark-robed figure is locked in silent combat with a pale one, who appears to be that strange man from the shadowy lane, though shadowed no longer. Their fight quickly takes them from my sight. Still, they could be back at any moment. I turn to warn the others, only to find their argument has grown so heated they are beyond noticing me.

Even Leal has joined in. "I do not know, my lady! I am only telling you what I have heard."

"Heard from whom? You heard it from your master. So, there is really no difference, is there?"

Lord Elden clenches his jaw. In the momentary silence, I finally have a chance to speak. "Does it really matter so much? We will find it all in time. But we are being watched and must get away from here *now*. Any direction is fine. We can figure the rest out later!"

"Giselle, I know you are afraid," Ami spits out. "But we cannot simply strike off blind like we have before. It's brought us nothing but misery, and we can't afford another fruitless day. We need a real plan or we won't last much longer in here."

Listening to this outburst, a vision swims unbidden to the front of my mind: the wood as it looked when I first saw it, a gently curving edge continuing out of sight on both sides, densely populated save for a small curved portion at the very edge of the horizon.

It's a wheel.

Yes! A wheel within a wheel. So, think. What does that mean?

That we must go...

"To the center," I declare with confidence.

"What was that?" Ami is taken aback by my seemingly pointless statement.

"The plan is to continue west to the center of the forest. There is a less dense space in the middle. I noticed it from the hilltop our second day out. Of course, from that distance there was no way to tell what the terrain is like. Perhaps rocky, perhaps not. But it's still our best chance. Surely, we'll find a river somewhere along the way. We've had fairly decent hunting so far, and the animals have to drink too."

Oh, well done.

"How can you be *sure*? We can't afford to waste time going the wrong way." Ami is fighting back tears now, obviously near her breaking point. One I've only seen her reach a handful of times in my life and would rather not witness again. When this girl loses it, bears run for cover. But her argument is wasting just as much time as walking the wrong way, and we must start somewhere.

I shrug, trying not to let the criticism sting. "I just am. This is my mind, remember? Now come on." I begin walking out of the dell in the opposite direction to the one we came. A quick glance back shows the others hesitating. "Come on!"

"She's right," Leal finally says, hurrying after me with Shadegleam.

With me leading away the supplies, and Leal at my heels, the others have no choice but to follow. We head due west, or as near west as we can figure in the maze of trees. I urgently search for the robed men as we walk, though I try to be covert about it. Relief floods me as I realize they haven't followed us.

The further from them we get, the more our tension starts to ease. Anger drains from Elden's face. Ami starts to sing a marching song and I join in. Shadegleam takes the longest to calm. The song is helping, but his ears are twitching again. I rub between them as I walk with Leal, softly singing till the tension leaves them both. Leal regains his status as Songmaster the moment Ami has finished.

The sun rises slowly. Some light manages to sift down through the treetops, and the cool breeze follows us from the dell. At first, I welcome the morning, delighting in the warmth of the few beams falling across my path. A wonderful day for a walk in the wood. Before long, however, the day warms back to its usual sweltering intensity. The air grows heavy and stale once more. All song stops as I struggle simply to draw enough air into my lungs. My pleasant walk in the wood has morphed into a death march through a smelting pot.

SWEAT POURS DOWN MY FACE, STINGING MY EYES. Wiping it off does no good. Our last stop was several hours ago, and I am in deep need of another. My legs ache, my lungs burn, my throat is parched. I understand now why Elden and Ami were so intent on planning a route. This heat is much worse than yesterday or the day before; the little water we have left will not last another. They haven't said a word, but I know they are thinking of it too. I hope I am not leading us all to death. No one knew the way, and someone had to make the hard choice, but I cannot help feeling that mine was a grievous error.

WATER. OH, HOW I WISH THERE WAS WATER. I CAN'T
see the trees before me any longer. Instead, I watch the
bubbling fountain at the home of the court physician,
the clear pool in which I used to play as a child, the swift
falls where I sat with Eamon not so long ago. Water, I
only want water! Even the light netting of the dreamsnare seems to burn me. Yet it is an odd, tingling
burning unlike anything I have felt before. The sensation draws me back, and I can see the trees once more.

Yes, I see the trees, but something else as well: a
faint glimmer not far off. The sweet music of water over
rocks drifts to my ears. Leal's shout is startling after so
long in the oppressive silence. He jumps on Shadegleam,
who perks up his ears and starts trotting toward the
miracle. We call for them to wait, but Leal doesn't pay
any heed, not even to his master. Grumbling, Elden
lights out after him. Ami and I follow close behind.

With every step, the music grows louder in my ears.
My hope soars. I have done it! I have led us right. I don't
stop at the water's edge but run full into the stream.
Spray washes my face as I stoop to draw a handful. I
know it is not wise to drink overmuch of a strange river
ere cleansing the water. I still cannot keep myself from
drinking. I stoop again and again. The water is shock-
ingly cold but sweet, gliding over my hands and down my
parched throat.

It's not till my thirst is appeased that I remember I
should be looking after the others. I see them further

downstream, laughing as they pour water over one another's heads. Well, it's really Ami and Leal who are mucking about. Elden just stands there, shaking his head and occasionally stepping out of range. Shadegleam prances about them, nickering and stomping the water in play.

No longer one to be left out, I sneak behind Ami and splash a good wave over her back. She shrieks, spinning to face me but stopping short of splashing. The world goes strangely still. Everyone is staring at me.

"Um...I'm sorry. Have I hurt you?"

"No, not at all!" But the reply comes too fast, too loud.

"Have I...done something...wrong?"

She begins to fidget with her hair again, eyes trained down on the water we have been seeking for so long.

"It is by no means you who is in the wrong, Lady Giselle." Elden's expression is so grave. Can't he ever have a bit of fun? "The fault lies with us."

"Well, then, what have you done?"

"I was angry with you," Ami whispers. "And then I doubted you when I had no right or reason to. I said I would follow you on this quest, and the first time I was asked to, I failed."

Leal sidles up next to me. "Well, I never did!"

Ami snorts and looks away from him.

"That's all?" I laugh. "Of course, you doubted me! I began to doubt myself. Now, it has turned out all right, so can we please put it behind us and enjoy this moment?"

Slowly, she grins and splashes me back. Leal joins us as we team up against Elden, who bows to the necessity of returning fire and makes for a vicious one-man army. At last, worn out and soaked to the skin, we set camp beside the life-giving river.

As I lie down to sleep, I sense the foreboding tingle in my spine once again. We are being watched. My eyes struggle open and I search for the robed men. I can see nothing in the inky blackness outside the fire's range. Not even the winking lights from this morning. I nervously draw out my talisman one last time. To my amazement, the black has receded. At midday a fourth of my time was gone. Now I can clearly see two of the most recently darkened strands cleared away. Yet I am so exhausted I can hardly comprehend the full impact, and my mind quickly drifts to other things. The last sight to meet my heavy eyes is that of Elden sitting wakeful by the fire, with Leal curled up next to him, fast asleep.

THE DANGER OF GEMS

An unnatural sound shatters my dream— something between a fierce growl and a pained shriek piercing the silent dark. I start and grope about me for a weapon, finding only a large stone. At first, I think the scream is Shadegleam's. He is going mad with fright, rearing and beating the air with his hooves, though he does not look injured. But then I make out a large, sleek figure retreating beyond the fire's pitiful glow. Elden stands by the dying embers, red-tinged sword held ready.

Ami is awake now, kneeling by my side. She clutches my arm with trembling hands. I do not believe I have ever seen her this pale before; of course, that could just be a trick of the poor light. And though Leal tries to put on a brave face, his fear cannot be mistaken. He is crouching behind Elden, clutching his bow with bone-white fingers. Shadegleam screams in terror and Leal moves to quiet him, but not quickly enough. The frantic horse breaks his picket and bolts into the night.

Elden spares a glance back, worry etched in every line of his face. His reaction disturbs me more than the blood-chilling cry of the beast or Shadegleam's terror. If he dealt a fatal blow, as I assume based on the animal's withdrawal, why does he look so?

Ami breathlessly asks, "Did you...kill it?"

I hold my breath for the answer.

"I fear not," he replies, the declaration hard and sharp as a knife edge. There is a rustling in the undergrowth, a rumor of movement on every side of us. Lord Elden turns his wary grey eyes back to the wood, searching for the cause of the disturbance. "He will return and will not come alone. These are creatures such as I have never seen. My stroke did the beast no great harm, though it was hard and quick enough to drop a raging warhorse. I fear these creatures cannot be overcome by my blade, though try I will. Nor do I see any chance of escape. Prepare yourselves!"

"Well, at least we get to see if all that combat training has paid off," I mutter under my breath.

A mad dash for weapons ensues, and, without quite knowing how it happened, I find myself waiting with a spear in hand and my back to the river. The fire, which Elden built up only enough to see clearly, burns as a shield before us. Ami is set slightly forward on my right. She loosens her stance and raises her spear, braced against her forearm, ready for a strike. I attempt to copy her but my knees are knocking with fright, and it's not long before my arms start shaking with the strain. So, I make do with a kneel, butt end of my spear planted firmly against the ground and tip pointing towards the danger.

The problem is...which way to point? I am surrounded by danger. I suppose it does not matter much. If the beasts truly can't be killed by a steel sword, this sharp stick isn't going to be much use. None of us are likely to last very long. Though I expect it will take a good deal to put Elden down. He stands the furthest out, slightly to the left of where the first creature vanished. Drawing up to his full stature, he adjusts his grip on the hilt of the sword, which glints a warning to any beast that dares approach.

Leal stands protectively in front of Ami, seemingly unconcerned that her spear tip is a handbreadth from his face. He complains when she gently pushes him aside.

"Leal, a bow is not the weapon for close combat," Elden reminds him. "We have but two spears left, and those the women must use. It would be best for you to cover us from above."

Leal is not altogether pleased, but he grudgingly agrees to the strategic move, quickly climbing a tree and waiting with his bow poised to shoot.

Time moves ever so slowly when one is awaiting something unpleasant. It seems an age that I have been standing here, though I know it is but a few moments, when the movement in the brush becomes more pronounced. One by one, strange pairs of eyes appear in the darkness, oddly shaped and brightly colored: red, blue, green, yellow, and white. They remind me of my dream in the dell last night. Though now I am beginning to think it was not a dream after all. They burn here and there, occasionally winking out but slowly growing in number and moving ever closer. Then the growling starts. My breath comes in loud, ragged gasps. I try hard to be quiet and not give myself away, but I cannot still my pounding heart. I grip my spear so tightly my arms begin to ache.

"I count six large beasts, my lord," Leal softly calls down. "They are wolves, I think."

His assertion puzzles me. Only wolves? That's not so bad. Dangerous, of course, but not uncommon in a wood. I had imagined much worse. Surely, Lord Elden has seen wolves before?

But when the foremost beast steps warily into the light, I understand. These wolves are not made of flesh. Wolves like gems, hewn gems of great size, brought to life by some sorcery. Ruby comes first, followed quickly by sapphire and emerald. Little wonder Elden is so ill at ease!

Their growling turns to howls, and the beasts charge, several at once.

"Beware!" Leal's cry rings out through the vicious din, an arrow accompanying it.

Battle is joined at last and I have no time for wonderment, only desperate action.

The ruby wolf bears down on me, and I adjust position, anchoring my spear more firmly against the ground. But as expected, the weapons that have served us well enough for hunting stand no chance against these beasts. That jarring first impact splinters my spear, leaving me with a large awkward cudgel. I roll aside and come up fumbling for the knife at my belt.

Jump left, quick.

One of Leal's arrows misses my shoulder by a hair-breadth and sinks deep in my opponent's side. Backing away from the enraged wolf, I spare a glance for the others. Elden strides boldly forward, dealing heavy blows that are met by equally heavy claws. Yet even as he lays his adversary low, it rises again, oozing a clear viscous substance I take to be blood. Ami is down to only a knife herself, but her determined expression is as fierce as the wolves'. Light on her feet, almost as if dancing, she twists and glides from the monsters' claws again and again, meting out swift jabs at unprotected flanks, throats, eyes, anything she can reach. Somehow, even with the chaos raging around me, I find time to admire her gracefulness and courage.

Forget her! You've got your own problems. Duck.

I, for one, am not dancing. In fact, I'm doing well just to avoid the razor-edged maw of my opponent without tripping. And that's only thanks to Haldis. If I had any lingering mistrust for her, it is quite gone now. I may not be as quick or graceful as Ami, but for once, I am grateful of my slight build. I can change course swifter than the beast I face at least, if nothing else.

We hold our ground for the moment. Still, we are surrounded by a pack of creatures whose injuries slow them but little. Whatever sorcery drives them keeps them standing longer than should be physically possible. And now diamond, topaz, and jade have joined the throng, fresh and full of bloodlust.

We have no sorcery to aid us and will not hold on much longer. I am so tired. My legs are lead, fixing me to the ground. My arms and back burn from the many slashes I have endured at the point of merciless claws. And I am fighting only one.

Ami is facing two together. Elden strides right up to the fire, warding off the remaining wolves with flaming brands. I *think* Leal is trying to fashion more arrows from tree branches, but I can't see him clearly. What exact use he thinks arrows without fletching, nock, or tip will be, only he can guess. He would get more use from throwing rocks, but for that he would have to leave the safety of the tree. At least he is trying something, which is more than can be said of me.

I know there isn't any chance of escape or even a moment of rest. We are hemmed in by the river. I try to accept my fate bravely. Take them down with me, like a true hero would.

Being foolish isn't the same as being a hero.

Swing left. Jump back. Duck right. Your other right, child!

I've always known I wouldn't manage the quest anyway. Might as well let go now and save everyone the trouble. I vaguely wonder again what will happen in my world if I die here. Will my friends be left waiting for me, wondering why I'm gone so long? Will Ami come home one day to find a corpse lying in her bed? No answer comes, and I haven't time to dwell on it. I know I will not last the night, but I might help my friends to see another sunrise.

It doesn't have to end that way. You were never one to give up. When did that change?

When I undertook a suicidal quest.

You're not helpless. You can do something about this. Just think.

Stumbling backward, I feel the cool river wash about my tired feet. The chill jolts me awake.

The river! We might be threatened by it, but so are they. Surely beasts as large and heavy as these will have trouble swimming in such a fast current, and I doubt their carven paws will stand firm on the wet rocks.

Now you are thinking. How can you lure them in?

I am paying more attention to the river than the

threat before me. As I step aside from the beast's lunge, I miss my footing and fall, losing my knife in the process. The monster draws in for the kill. I scramble aside and my hand meets my discarded cudgel. I raise it not a moment too soon, shoving it between the wolf's snapping jaws and pushing upwards with all my strength.

Suddenly, a new sound mixes with the pounding of blood in my ears and the snarling of the beast above me. It takes me a moment to realize the thrumming is that of hooves. Shadegleam has returned! He falls upon the beast, toppling them both far out into the water. Now my assumption is proven true, at least in part. The wolf does indeed find his footing hard to master. But though he flounders for a moment, with his massive legs scrabbling and slipping on the riverbed, the water is not as deep nor as quick as I thought. Not enough to drown them, and how could we possibly out-swim them? Even a strong horse like Shadegleam can't carry us all, and he is having trouble keeping himself upright against the current as well.

The hope, so swiftly born within me, dies in an instant. My heart is quite as heavy as the next adversary I turn to face. If only the river were a bit deeper, a bit quicker. If only there were a barge, a raft, a boat, something to ferry us away. If only...

Yes, yes, you need a faster current.

But there isn't one!

Make one. Use your talisman.

Use the talisman? I thought its purpose was to protect my mind, which it apparently does of its own accord.

It is much more complex than you think. And you've used it before.

Did I?

You found this river when you needed it, so quickly, almost as if you made it. Remember? Use the talisman.

I'm still not sure what she's talking about, but I'm desperate enough to try anything. "Very well then," I whisper, as if giving voice to my reply will work some magic, "how do I use it?"

I told you. Just think. Think hard.

So, I do. I put all my energy into envisioning a deep, swift river and a barge to ply it. The dreamsnare burns hot against me, bringing me to my knees in pain. A pain I hardly notice once I see the black burning off the strands far faster than it climbed on. And in that same moment, the river does just as I was wishing.

The wolf Shadegleam faced off with howls as the river rushes around him, deepening and quickening until he is drawn under. A thunderous crash can be heard above the water's roar. A great cedar tree has fallen lengthwise into the river, a ship riding the foam to collect us.

Well done. Very well done!

All thanks to you!

The others are so consumed with avoiding claw and fang that they have yet to notice this spectacle.

"The river," I call as loud as I can, trying to be heard above the cacophony of war and flood. "Ami, Elden, run to the river. Leal, leave that and come down."

There is no time now to explain my plan; I must simply trust them to follow. They turn as I wade out to meet our salvation. The current pulls at my legs, nearly dragging me in as well. Luckily, the tree is pushed with so much force it wedges deep into the bank, giving us time to climb up. Leal is there before the others, helping me get supplies onboard.

The vessel is relatively bare and flat on top, as if it had been sheared off on one side by some great force before it fell. That should provide us a safe place to sit, though reaching it is proving a challenge thanks to the odd angle and sticky resin. I finally haul myself up and lay still a moment to catch my breath. As I turn to help the others, I see Shadegleam struggling onto the far bank. I was worried when the river rose so quickly with him still mid-stream, but he snorts good-naturedly and trots toward someone just within the tree line. It's too dark to see who, whether the pale man or the dark or someone else entirely. A shiver runs down my back, but I stifle the dread. I simply haven't the leisure to worry about something that is not an immediate threat.

Ami climbs up right behind me, lugging both my pack and her own. Elden has hung back to defend our escape. The current is pulling at the tree so forcefully it is all I can do to keep my seat.

"Now, Elden! This won't stay put much longer."

Finally, he turns from the wolves and races to the tree. He catches a branch and deftly weaves his way up. We drag him aboard just as the bark is violently wrenched from its hold on the shore.

Wolves race one another into the water, trying to catch us as we speed away. There is a pileup on the bank now, a few smart ones trying to go back while others come in. Most are drowning, but a few of those furthest back turn and flee into the wood. I don't see the wolves' end. We are traveling too fast, and they are soon out of sight. While my companions are still distracted, I draw out my dreamsnare once more. Only a fraction of the dark is left. The burnt strands have been fully restored!

Ami stares open mouthed at the water rushing below us for a solid five minutes and then begins laughing. "I can't decide if this is genius or madness! We escaped the wolves but are in danger of drowning any minute."

The tree tilts slightly to the right, as if to punctuate her words. But the weight of the limbs below act as a counterbalance and we are not thrown off. I sigh in relief.

Elden chuckles. "Let us not disparage this chance the Greatest Power has sent us. We are safe enough." He turns to regard me with warm eyes. "You did remarkably well tonight, Giselle. You held your own in combat, showed quick wit, and a great deal of pluck. I couldn't have hoped for better."

I feel my cheeks burning red and hope it is still too dark for him to notice. "Well, that is taking it a bit far, but uh...thank you. Thank you, Lord Elden."

"Really, Giselle." Ami's voice drips annoyance. I could swear she rolls her eyes. "Just take the compliment. You deserve it."

"You too surpassed my expectations, Lady Ami." Elden offers. "Your fighting has improved considerably."

"It really has," Leal pipes up. "I've never seen a girl fight like that!"

Elden snorts. "Only because I have taken great care to keep you away from the Blades. Best for chattering young boys to avoid women with swords."

"Well, I bet Lady Ami could join and best the lot of them," Leal retorts.

She laughs, ruffling his hair. He takes great care to straighten it back.

"We all did well," she replies then stifles a yawn. "Now, I'm going to finish my sleep. It's too dark for any other useful employment. Even patching wounds correctly will have to wait. I'm sorry, but it's not safe to light a torch and I can't see well enough for delicate work. We'll wrap the worst and I'll have a good look at first light."

I lean back against an irregular branch with my cloak spread over me and close my eyes. But my mind is buzzing now. All the worries of the past few days bombard me. The men following us, the wolves, my dreamsnare's new developments, and what if the tree does roll in the night? After an hour of unproductive and uncomfortable fidgeting, I sit back up and watch the sun slowly rise over the water, illuminating our wake as we glide along.

❧ 12 ❧

A POWERFUL TALISMAN

I grit my teeth as Ami cleans and bandages my wounds. I don't know what she's put on the gashes across my back, but it stings worse than a whole hive of agitated bees. And unfortunately, I do know exactly what that feels like. Several years ago, during one of his rare excursions to the countryside, Uncle got it into his head we should gather wild honey. By which he meant I was to gather the honey, of course. That was a hard one to hide from Ami and Gil.

"Do try not to squirm. I know it's horrid, but that means the treatment is working. It'll be over soon, I promise."

Leal wiggles his fingers, caught tightly in mine. Ever the misguided gentleman, he insisted since he hasn't got any injuries, I ought to hold his hand while mine are seen to. I'm sure he's regretting it now.

"There, I'm done. Just lie still for a bit and you'll feel better."

"Thank you," I manage faintly.

"Now, Lord Elden, let me have a look at you."

He really should have been treated first, having borne the brunt of the fighting. But he claimed he was the most accustomed to battle injury and refused to be helped until we were safely seen to. He moans a few times as Ami sews up some nasty cuts, but somehow sits still as stone.

"That's finished, Lord Elden," Ami sighs well over an hour later. "You are lucky my mother trained me before her death. She taught me many things other healers have never known. I only hope it is enough."

"I thank you, good lady. You needn't fret. I have lived through much worse than this."

"Have we, my lord?" Leal mutters. I've never heard him use such an ironic tone with his master before. He must be in a really foul mood to risk it, but Elden simply lies back and closes his eyes.

Ami has fallen asleep again and Elden rests fitfully. The sun is bright and hot above us, sapping my energy further. After our active night and my inability to sleep this morning, I could easily nod off, but I know what a bad idea that is. Leal seems to have boundless energy now that he has woken, and he has no wounds to hamper his movement. Though one would expect a boy of nine years capable of looking after himself, I've seen enough of his impulsivity not to trust him alone.

"Leal, will you please sit still for five minutes?" He's swinging between the few limbs not underwater, headed toward the front of the tree.

"But, Lady Giselle, I've got to make more arrows. And since there might not be a chance later, I better make good use of our time now. There ought to be some decent limbs nearer the top that I can use for shafts."

"Oh, very well. Just pick your footing carefully. It isn't safe moving around on this thing and I don't want you pitched into the water."

"Aww, don't fret, Lady Giselle. I'm the best at tree climbing!" He scampers off before I can change my mind.

"That might be, but have you ever climbed a tree while it rushes on its side down a river?" I call after him.

He doesn't answer. I can't see where he goes except for a slight rustling of branches here and there as he moves about. I don't mean to, but I do eventually nod off. The shouting wakes me hours later.

"Mind the packs, boy! You've nearly sent them into the river."

"I'm terribly sorry, my lord. I only meant to get my fishing line out."

"What use have you for a fishing line now?"

"I'm hungry. And it will save some of the food."

Elden takes a deep breath and closes his eyes for

several moments before answering. "Leal," he speaks very slowly, "look around you. Is this a still lake? Do we have any means of directing our course to find an advantageous fishing hole?"

"Well, not really."

"Correct. The river is much too quick for a catch here. Moreover, there is no way for us to prepare the fish. We can't very easily light a fire, can we? Put the line away and go sit down."

Leal throws his line down, snagging it hopelessly around several branches in the process, and storms to the farthest side of the vessel.

"Don't go too far out, Leal," Ami calls then turns on Elden. "Must you be so hard on him?"

"He was only trying to help." That boy might drive me crazy, but for some reason, I still find myself defending him.

"He generally is, but he must learn some sense quickly if he wants to survive as a knight."

Ami huffs as she turns and follows Leal. Elden sighs and hunches over. "But I ought to have kept my temper." He looks positively dejected.

Seeing him so miserable makes me feel a bit guilty. I didn't have a right to reprimand him. He's just trying to keep us all alive. I'm the one that fell asleep and left Leal unsupervised, after all.

"It isn't your fault. Everyone is tired, and Leal simply isn't very good at sitting still."

"No. I must remember he is only a boy."

Elden has hardly finished speaking when we hear a loud splash.

"Oh dear."

"Leal! What have you done now?"

"It's all right. I'm all right, my lord. I can get back on."

༺❀༻

A JOLT NEARLY TOPPLES ME HEADFIRST INTO THE freezing water. The flooded river has slowed to a gently flowing stream, causing our unwieldy raft to finally stick fast—and just in the nick of time, too. With tempers running as short as they have been after another night in the tree, someone would likely have found themselves a watery grave before the end of the day.

I groan as my stiff legs protest the effort of clambering down. Elden has already descended and reaches up to help me the last bit. Leal is sluggishly hauling the waterlogged packs up the bank. Even his energy has run its course. Ami refuses Elden's aid and alights beside me, gracefully, yet with such a scowl on her face I want to laugh. It is clear she is feeling no better than the rest of us.

"Ugh. I am ever so glad to be rid of that perch. I'm not a bird and don't take kindly to sleeping in treetops," she grumbles.

Elden's ill-tempered guffaw rings through the brisk morning air. "Deliverance from death at the jaws of jeweled beasts is not enough. Nay, next time we shall build a magnificent ship to elude them. Would that be more to your satisfaction?"

"Hold your tongue!" The glare she trains on him would have stopped one of the gem wolves in its tracks. "I was only jesting."

Elden gives her a stiff bow. "Forgive me, I am not in the best of dispositions at the moment. Though I was also in jest, I ought not to have spoken so forcefully." His clipped words belie his respectful gesture.

Time to put my mediator skills to use. "I don't think anyone would be in good spirits after everything we've been through. I am grateful for our safety but certainly do not want to do that again anytime soon."

"It wasn't all that bad," Leal chirps, his irrepressible good will already returned by contact with solid ground. "And it saved us at least a day's walk!" Leave the optimism to Leal and you'll never run out.

We gather around the packs and begin to take stock of our meager possessions. There was quite a lot left behind during the fight and more was lost to the river. As I empty packs and sort piles, I think of my talisman. It obeyed my command to save us, perhaps it can replenish some of our lack. But will it produce anything I ask or only certain things? Does it have a limit?

A muted oath draws me back to the task at hand.

Elden has pulled his sword from its scabbard, intending to give it a proper cleaning now that he has the stability to do so. However, the sword is far beyond help. He holds a mangled wreck of steel, badly dented and the tip broken. It is still loosely fixed to the bloodied hilt, but a deep crack runs just underneath.

"This will not be of any use now! At the least, the hilt may be cleaned and come in useful later, yet I see little hope of re-forging the blade. Nor can I obtain a new sword till I reach my post."

"We have hardly any weapons left," I whisper. I did not mean for anyone to hear; Elden is in a foul enough temper already. Just my luck.

"I still have my bow," Leal replies. "I'll make you one too. And I can help Lord Elden make more spears."

Elden shakes his head in disbelief. "The spears we can do, Leal, but only in your dreams do we have the time and ability to properly season and fashion bow-staves."

In our dreams. I think of my dreamsnare again. If I can truly make whatever I like with it, I could get us a few decent weapons. I just need time to figure out how it works. But we don't have that time now. When the inspection is finished, we find that Ami has lost a water-skin. And turns out, it wasn't hers.

"The one I lent you?" Elden speaks through his teeth. "Not that it matters which. Do you not know how deeply we are in need of them all? There is no telling how long we may go before finding the next water source."

"I know. I do, and I am sorry. All right? I'm sorry! You needn't reprimand me. You are not the only one who is worried."

"It was not her fault, my lord," Leal interjects. "I was helping to pack the bags and misplaced it."

Elden gives an exasperated grunt and begins intently cleaning what is left of his mangled sword.

"No, Leal," Ami says sternly, "you did not."

"Lady Ami," he whispers, "I'm helping."

"You really are not. I don't need you to take blame for me. Certainly not from Lord Elden."

Just as we are repacking and about ready to set off, there is a scuffling among the trees nearby. All bickering stops as the sound grows louder. First, I think it is one of the wolves, but they could not have possibly followed our trail. Then, I fear it is whoever or whatever has been watching us since we first set foot in the forest. I have not caught sight of the menacing dark-cloaked man since we left the dell with the oak. However, there is still that pale-robed stranger, and I'm not sure I trust him any more than the other.

The branches part and out trots a horse. A horse dark as midnight shadows. I catch a glimpse of pale robes behind him, but when I look, there is no one there. My exhausted mind must be playing tricks on me. "Shadegleam," I cry and rush to grab his bridle, Leal right behind me. I don't know much about horses, but he shows me how to determine whether there are any serious injuries.

"Shadegleam?" Elden sputters. "That is not his name. You cannot simply rename my horse!"

"But he likes it. Don't you, Shadegleam? I was worried for you."

The horse whinnies and tosses his head.

"It's a good name." Ami backs me up, though I'm not so sure she does it out of friendship for me but simply to get at Elden. If so, it has the desired effect.

"Confound women! One loses my best waterskin and the other not only demolishes my horse's good name but steals his affection as well."

"What is his name then?"

"No matter. Shadegleam it is now. I must say I do agree with the Lady Amita in one respect," he grudgingly informs us. "You have named him well." He ties the four remaining packs to the horse's back and decidedly turns away from us all. "Come along then, *Shadegleam*. We had better get a start before the day wastes entirely away."

❧

I walk in the rear this time. It gives me a clearer path and a chance to inspect my talisman unobserved. It looks just the same as before. Simple fisherman's netting, hanging downward from the metal ring fixed to the twine around my neck. Only a small amount of black is left, allowing me to breathe easier for now. There is nothing else to mark it as magical or significant in any way. Perhaps that is just as well; no one will think to take it from me. Now, how does it work? Do I need to only wish for something hard enough? I doubt it but try anyway. "I wish for a new waterskin," I whisper. Nothing, not even a slight warmth in the metal.

Well, it could be a talisman only for protection. We seem to have always been in bad situations when I used it before. Perhaps I must wish for something protective. Gathering the netting into my fist, I grip it hard, close my eyes, and think with all my might. "A sword! We need a sword. Please, please, give me a new sword for Lord Elden." I open my eyes. Once again, nothing has happened.

"Well," I exclaim to the uncaring talisman, "that is very inconsiderate. I think I'll—"

"He is not truly angry," a young voice sounds right beside me. "At least, he will not be for long."

I start and look up. For once Leal was quiet enough I didn't hear him drop back to walk with me. Elden, however, is well ahead.

"He meant it more in jest, I am sure. You don't need to hide back here. I think he is actually quite pleased. About the horse, you know. He always says horses are a better judge of character than most men."

"I'm not hiding," I reply. "I'm only a bit tired."

Ami hears us and looks back, inspecting me as she slows to join us. "Hmm...as you like. What is that?" She points to my hand.

I start to hide my prize.

Ask her. She ought to know a great deal about how magic and talismans work here.

Do you always have to butt in? I'm sure I can do this one myself.

Giselle.

Fine!

So, instead of withdrawing my hand, I stretch it out towards Ami. "It is called a dreamsnare." I quickly explain everything I know about it, including the Time-piece of Doom function, which she takes remarkably well. "Only, I can't figure out how to work it." I end with a rueful glance down at the offending object.

Ami's face brightens. She immediately launches into a lecture on the differences between talismans and their multitudinous uses, losing me within the first few sentences. "...different kinds of protection. Yours gives you mental protection. I would say it not only catches intruders but also responds to mental actions the intruders would inhibit. Imagining, planning, devising strategy...of course, that aspect only works properly in life-threatening situations, in holding with the protective qualities of the talisman."

I concentrate, trying to understand all the complicated criteria she has just spouted off. "It led us to the river because we were desperate for water and I was thinking about fountains? And then the flood came only because I had figured out a way to defeat the wolves."

"Precisely. Though, I think it's possible the talisman created the river in the first place."

"I don't suppose there is a reasonably safe way to test it. It truly only works for the difference of life and death?"

"Yes."

"Surely you will have opportunity to test it before long. We are certain to be in need of your genius again soon!" Leal seems under the impression that I enjoy near death experiences.

Ami almost laughs. "Let's hope we don't need it often. The good news, however, is that it appears to utilize energy from this Devoron when up against a large task. That would be why some strands cleared off. So, at least death traps can buy us more time in the long run."

That isn't as encouraging as she attempts to make it sound.

"And if our previous experiences are not enough to convince you, I am not sure another will have much more impact. Why, in the past two days alone, we have been stalked, nearly died of thirst, were attacked by strange wolves of gemstone, and spent a day and night on the river in a very unwieldy transport. Why, today has been a perfect holiday in comparison. But then, we *are* due for another adventure. I do hope it is an especially thrilling one!"

I laugh at the feigned excitement in her voice. She must be even more apprehensive than I am. "Of course you do." I replace the dreamsnare around my neck, concealing it beneath my tunic. We hurry to catch up with Elden, who is now out of sight but left a clear path to follow.

❧ 13 ❧

A MYSTERIOUS PAST

L eal says Elden isn't truly angry about the horse's name, and he would be the one to know. Still, I feel that I ought to at least attempt an apology. I come up alongside him, squeezing between two large trees and stumbling over a root in the process. He puts out a hand to steady me. Though his touch does not linger, the simple connection recalls that odd feeling we have met before. The pesky musings resurface, and I give my head a subtle shake. I don't need this distraction right now.

"I really am sorry," I venture.

"Sorry? What have you got to be sorry for? Your quick thinking saved our lives."

Has he already forgotten? Then I probably shouldn't bring it up again. But the reply spews from my mouth before I can stop it. "About naming your horse against your wishes."

"Ah, that." He pauses for a moment, his head hanging low. "It is I who should apologize to you for my unknightly conduct, and to the Lady Ami also. To tell truly, I do not much care what the horse is called. I was only in a foul temper and liable to put an ill face on anything." He stands straight again and smiles, cheeks slightly red. "I am very pleased to find how much you like him. He has assuredly taken a liking to you."

I smile back, with less caution than I have before. "What was his name?"

"It is of small consequence. I see no reason for you to be bothered with it."

"Please, I really would like to know."

"If it would please you so much, I'll not withhold it. His name was Warmund."

"Warmund. That's not a bad name."

"I thought not, though Shadegleam is much better."

I duck my head, tucking a strand of hair behind my ear. We are essentially alone now, as Ami and Leal are deep in discussion some distance behind us. I can hear his exuberant voice telling one story after another of Elden's Great Deeds, as he calls them. The current one apparently being the day they met. "I was in deep trouble, I can tell you. But then my Lord Elden came out of an alley and saw them. He fought off all five at once..."

They are too preoccupied to notice anything we might say. I suppose now is as good a time as any to try and clear up my conflicting feelings towards Elden. I attempt to sound casual as I pry into his past. "Well then, Lord Elden, where do you and Warmund, and Leal, of course, come from?"

"Shadegleam and Leal have come with me from the kingdom of Ivlin."

Ivlin? That was Healer Aliza's birthplace! "I have heard tell of Ivlin, though I don't know much of it. What sort of place is it?"

"The very best of places. Second only to the Ivory Isle, which is said to be enchanted to perfection by the Creative One himself. In summer, the fountains run with water as of gold, and in winter, they freeze not, but turn all to silver crystals. The towers of pearl gleam in their own light, though not as bright as that which comes from the isle across the sea. The hearth is never permitted to burn out."

Leal's voice drifts to me again. "He brought me to his home in Ivlin. He even made me his page and provided lodging in the room next to his. It is a wonderful place, Ivlin! Much nicer than my old home..."

"It sounds lovely, Lord Elden," I reply a bit wistfully. "What caused you to leave?"

He sighs. "There is a war on and a post to fill. All must play their part, much as I may regret mine."

"You spoke of a post earlier. I hope lending us aid will not cause you too much trouble."

"You will never be too much trouble." His expression as he says it warms me in a way I know it shouldn't, especially not with Eamon waiting for me at home, but I'm not given time to examine my wayward heart as he gruffly clears his throat and continues. "I have been sent as ambassador to the dwarves for a twelvemonth and two. It is not a repulsive job. I have attended the forges at home in my spare time. Not an altogether proper occupation for a noble, I know, but I rather enjoy crafting. I believe it is good for all men to know a skill, regardless of their status." He chuckles at some private joke. "And it did me no harm when befriending my fellow knights."

"Then why do you act as if you are dreading this assignment?"

"It is the dwarves themselves. They may well prove my bane. This quest has been a good bit of luck!"

I laugh outright. "I would not call it lucky, but I am glad to be of service for once."

"It is most welcome."

"But what is so grievous about the dwarves?"

"I ought not speak ill of our allies. For staunch allies they have been. Yet, I find dwarves too close-minded. They are swift to pass judgment and the punishment is often more severe than the crime warrants."

"I see. And you are worried you will make a mistake and receive an unfair sentence?"

"Not quite. I must remain in the dwarven king's good

graces if we are to obtain the needed weapons, and that may result in partaking of some very unpleasant tasks. In short, I fear I will be forced to pass too harsh a sentence on another. Or at best, stand by and watch it happen."

"Are you certain you are a noble?" I quip. "They are not nearly so kindhearted."

"Perhaps." His voice has dropped, and his face reddens again as he looks away. It takes a few seconds, but he is smiling when he continues. "Or perhaps it is only that the noblemen of your country are undeserving of their title. I am not so different from others in Ivlin."

The conversation lapses as we trudge on. I do not know what Elden's mind is occupied with—possibly longing for his home. I know I would be homesick if sent away from such a wonderful land and ponder what my life in a country like Ivlin could be. In this pause, Leal and Ami's discussion can be heard more clearly.

"...and so, I went to work at the inn. I don't much like it, but you can see I had no choice really."

"Why, that's absolutely terrible, Lady Ami. When we return, I will challenge them all to a duel!"

"I appreciate the sentiment, Leal," Ami responds dryly, "but there is really no need for that."

"No, I suppose you can defeat them all yourself." He finally quiets down but not for long. "Here, I have an idea! You mustn't tell anyone till I am certain of being right."

"And...what is this idea?" Ami sounds reasonably

TO SLAY A CURSE

apprehensive. There's no telling what he will come up with next.

Leal tries to lower his voice, something at which he does not exactly excel. "I do believe my master is greatly taken with the Lady Giselle. Isn't it wonderful? She is very nice and will be a good match for him."

"Oh, really. And how do you reckon that?"

"He has been much happier on this quest than I have seen him in a long time. He doesn't show it much, but I can tell. Also, I have seen something in his pack..."

I stumble and right myself before Elden notices. Trying not to look at him, I take a few steps away. He coughs loudly and begins another conversation, asking about my home this time. The little light we have is fading now and the wind is picking up. It must be a perfect gale up there to blow so hard this far below the treetops. I shiver and wrap my arms around myself. Unfortunately, my cloak was in tatters after the wolves and suitable for nothing more than bandages. I don't have another.

Elden pulls something from his pack at Shadegleam's side. He holds it out to me while clearing his throat roughly. "Here, take this."

"See, Lady Ami. That was most certainly not in his pack before we met." Leal is quite pleased with himself.

I take the shawl, holding it gently as if it will disappear at any moment. It should not be here. The last time I saw this, it was only made of shadow, an image in the mist on a back lane. My tenth birthday present. How does Elden have it?

"Where did you get this?" It tumbles from my lips before I can stop it. Not an appropriate response at all. Blushing, I quickly add my thanks.

He shrugs and begins walking faster. "I saw it while gathering supplies at the market. I thought, traveling with two ladies, it was sure to prove useful."

"Oh...I see." Not just for me then. Of course not. "Well, thank you."

"You are most welcome."

As I wrap the warm shawl about me, I realize who Elden reminds me of so strongly. I still cannot explain his resemblance to the strange man always on the edge of my consciousness, but I know for sure who Elden is. Odd that only with this realization do I understand who gave me the shawl so long ago: Eamon. I suppose my heart has not wandered after all.

⚜

WE FINALLY MAKE CAMP FOR THE NIGHT. AMI AND I have taken a chance in lying farther from the fire, and the men, so that we may talk in private.

"I have learned a great deal today," Ami says.

"Have you? So have I."

"You do not look overly happy about it. What is wrong?"

I sigh. "Do you remember what I told you at the inn, about my real world?"

"Yes, certainly!"

"Do you remember what I told you...of Eamon?"

She smiles smugly and nudges me with her elbow. "Why, who could forget him?"

"Yes, who indeed?" Though I seem to have quite easily. "Well, I just realized that he has a double here also. But Lord Elden doesn't know who he is. He doesn't know me."

Ami laughs outright. "Giselle, honestly, you needn't worry. Leal has been telling me quite a lot about his master today."

"Yes, so I heard. Some of it, at least. How Eamon, I mean Elden, rescued him and took him to Ivlin as his page."

"Yes, but there was more. He is convinced Elden has feelings for you. I am inclined to agree."

"I heard that too, but he must be mistaken. Like I said, he doesn't know me. And despite traveling so far together, we have barely ever spoken until today. So, how can he care for me?"

Ami shakes her head. "Oh, Giselle! For this brilliant mind you have, one that seemingly created an entire living world, you can be quite dense. Elden isn't one to talk much, but that doesn't mean he hasn't got eyes. Quite nice eyes, in fact. And you have no idea how often they watch you when he thinks no one is looking."

"Oh, that's just fine then. He looks at me when he doesn't want to be seen. But he talks to you in the open all the time. And if this is a beauty contest, you win hands down."

Ami rubs between her eyes and groans. "You must stop being so hard on yourself. It's giving me a headache."

"But—"

"We don't talk, Giselle, we argue. There is a big difference. Believe it or not, even warriors don't like being in conflict all the time. And don't ever try to tell me you aren't pretty. Besides, that's not even what I was referring to. Think about it. The man has seen you willing to take a beating for me, carry twice your share of the packs whenever you can get away with it, hold your own against monsters three times your size, and save us all from a gruesome death with a very unforgettable escape. You really don't think that's enough of a reason for him to like you? All right then, add in that you obviously care about Leal and his horse just as much as he does, and it's all set."

"Yeah, still not sure that's how a great relationship is developed, Ami."

"Don't worry, all right? It will all work out in the end. Trust me. And if not...well, you'll still have your man waiting when you go home, right? Now, we better get some sleep before we are attacked again."

"Perhaps we will make it through the night safely this time."

"Doubtful, but perhaps. Oh, there was one thing I forgot to tell you. Leal says that his name is only one he received when he joined Lord Elden's family. His given name is Gilpin."

"Gilpin." I laugh. "Well, that explains so much."

"Yes. No wonder the boy won't leave me alone." She chuckles. "Good night, Giselle dear."

"Good night."

❧ 14 ☙

BUDS, BLOSSOMS, AND BLAZE

The dawn brings with it a rare chorus of songbirds, and I lie a moment delighting in the novelty. Though I rise with the birds, I find I am the last one to wake.

"Good morning, Ami." I join her breakfast preparations.

"Morning, Giselle."

"Oh, bacon!"

"The last of it."

"Still, sunshine, songbirds, *and* bacon? Looks like our luck is turning."

"Not for long, I'll warrant," Elden grumbles as he stoops down to put his pack in order.

"Oh, naturally," Ami replies ironically. "This wood won't leave us in peace for long. Something dreadful is bound to happen soon." Then she looks at me out the corner of her eye and continues, "Although, that surely doesn't mean something wonderful could not happen as well."

Avoiding Elden's eyes, I inspect my shawl. It is slipping and I take great care in adjusting it, brushing off the specks of grass that have migrated during the night. "So, um, where...where's Leal?" I try to speak evenly, though I am very aware that the heat in my face is showing through.

"Oh, that creature of boundless energy is up a tree." Ami says it as if I ought to have guessed already.

"What, again?"

"Yes, again." Elden gazes upwards at a nearby beech. "It seems my page has taken to giving orders. I suppose I shall have to do something about that," he muses good-naturedly. "He announced very early this morning that we could not possibly continue ere he had replenished his quiver and promptly disappeared among the leaves."

"Well, you certainly cannot deny we need more weapons."

"No, I do not deny it. I only object to a lengthy delay," he replies, then adds in an undertone, "and to my page giving me orders."

Just then, Leal comes scrambling down the tree trunk, a fistful of sharpened sticks clutched in one hand. He drops to the ground in a heap and begins running towards us. "I have plenty of shafts. I only need to fix the fletching. It will not take long, master. I promise."

"Leal, we have not the time for you to hunt and pluck a few birds. The arrows will have to wait."

"Oh, but I have a pouch full already. See here?" Leal opens a pouch tied at his belt. Inside is a small roll of twine and an abundance of downy feathers. Then he turns to me and holds out a small fat bit of wood with a shard of flint attached, roughly chipped along the edges and about the size of my previous dagger. "Here, Lady Giselle, I made this for you. Not overly fine, but it should do in a scrape."

"Why, uh...thank you, Leal. Where did you..." I tentatively reach out and take the 'dagger.'

"Oh, I found the flint on the riverbank yesterday. I've got a few more, but it will take a while to get them into shape. Well then, I better get these arrows finished. Come on, Lady Ami, I need your help!" He grabs her hand and pulls her off among the trees.

"Aye, finish it then," Elden calls after him. "Just see you are back within the hour." But they have already disappeared. He sighs and shakes his head. "Sometimes I regret taking that boy on. But then he always does something to cheer me."

"You've done well with him. He is a fine boy and quite devoted to you."

"A devoted page, he is. But alas, devotion does not always translate to competency."

"I suppose that's true." I look down and wrap the

shawl closer about me. "Thank you again for this shawl. You needn't have gotten such a fine one."

He smiles and shrugs. "I am glad to put it to use. Just as I am glad you have a weapon again. I had intended to lend you my spare dagger till such time as I can make new spears, but now without my sword..." He lets the sentence hang. "And, after all, even flint is better than nothing."

"Yes, well, I am sure he meant well, but I won't be able to use it. I could barely use the spear and am even worse with close combat. I'm beginning to think I won't be much use in a fight, no matter how much training you put me through."

He grins. "You should not be so hard on yourself. You have improved a good deal from when we first met. Rather, say that it is my fault for always pitting you against the boy. However, as there is no such thing as overtraining, and we are alone..." He trails into silence, but it's not hard to get what he's driving at.

"If I agree, will you let me out of this evening's training?"

He quirks an eyebrow, grin growing wider. "Not a chance! Did I not just say there is no such thing as over-training?"

"A proper taskmaster, you are." I *tsk*, crossing my arms and turning up my nose. "Ought to be ashamed of yourself."

Elden laughs heartily at that.

An answering smile tugs at the corners of my pout and I can't maintain the pretense any longer. Chuckling, I nod toward the dagger at his hip. "Go on, then."

The next hour is filled with nothing but sweat and bruises. We have a few good laughs at my failures. Lucky thing Elden is such a patient teacher. He sometimes needs to direct my hand in demonstration but is careful to hold on no longer than necessity requires and still makes me do most of the work.

Once I can perform the new strikes correctly, Elden stands opposite and instructs me to fight him. This is much more difficult and the source of most of the bruising. He constantly reminds me to strike harder and move faster. It doesn't help that much of this sparring puts us in positions that would certainly be outside the bounds of propriety if we were at home. Not that I mind, but it does my concentration no favors.

When I lose my knife to him for the fifth time in a row, he calls a truce.

"That is enough for the present. You have done exceedingly well for such a short time."

Refusing to grow flustered at every compliment, I nod with a grateful smile. "Thank you, but it's due to your teaching. I only hope I can remember it all when needed."

He lays a comforting hand on my shoulder. "You will."

I open my mouth to reply but am interrupted by the

others' return. Ami's eyebrows shoot up when she sees us. My face grows warm as I realize what this must look like. Elden and I standing inches apart, still slightly out of breath and our clothes disarranged. He snatches his hand back and I take a small step away, but Ami has already begun eyeing the distance between us with a grin.

"Are you two still not ready?" She laughs. "And here I was thinking we'd get a good tongue lashing for being late. What do you think, Leal, should we leave them alone a bit longer?"

"Oh, shut up, Ami." I brush past her to get my pack.

WE HAVE BEEN MARCHING FOR HOURS WITH FEW stops, much like any other day. And much like any other day, it is exceedingly hot. I had blissfully, temporarily forgotten my dreamsnare and did not check it this morning. When I do now, I see that the black has climbed incredibly fast and is already nearly equal what it was before escaping the wolves. My heart plummets, and I have not even the birdsong to cheer me now. In fact, I have neither heard nor seen any animal in several hours. And my inky little friends haven't shown in days. I'm beginning to think we lost them at the river along with the wolves.

Even Leal has been unusually quiet, but he suddenly rectifies that. "Bless me, can you smell that?"

I hadn't noticed till he mentioned it, but the air has certainly changed. There is a hint of something fresh and sweet not far off. Now that I know it's there, it grows stronger with each breath, laying hold of my mind. I can't help taking an especially deep breath, attempting to hoard as much of the lovely smell as I can. Oh, it is so very sweet. Bewitchingly so.

"What is that?" I ask no one in particular.

Be wary. The scent bears a strain of enchantment. Mayhap with no malevolent intent, but it does not bode well, all the same. No matter how pleasant it might seem.

"Where's it coming from?" Leal is in a tizzy, spinning like a top as he searches for the source.

"I think it is off that way. To the left. Do let's find it. It's about time for a rest anyway," Ami pleads.

"But shouldn't we stay on course?" I would love to go, but I must also heed Haldis' warning. And I am not so sure we will be able to find our way back if we wander off now.

"What course?" Ami puts her hands on her hips. "Giselle, we haven't *got* a course."

"Yes, we do. West. That's our course."

"West. Yes, you keep saying that. West. But do you even know for certain that we are going west? It's impossible to tell direction in here. There is not a road to follow. We are only guessing at the way to begin with. And just think what we might find!"

"Yes, and that is what worries me."

"I stand with Lady Giselle. It is not advisable to wander off. We truly haven't the time nor the resources for another detour." Elden is technically the leader, but Ami never listens to him, and this time even Leal is too far gone to follow orders.

"We are already lost, my lord. What harm can it do? Please, mightn't we go?"

"We are not lost, Leal. Do you truly think I have not even the skill to tell direction from things other than the sun?"

Leal holds back tears as he begs Elden again. The aroma is indeed very powerful. He's still a boy, I remind myself, and this has been a very hard journey. Ami, on the other hand, really ought to be behaving better. Instead, she has let the beguiling scent fully draw her into its grasp.

It takes a great deal of effort, but I remain free. At least my years of struggle against Devoron have accomplished something good. Elden, too, seems a bit more clearheaded than the rest of us. Noblemen must go through some form of training to withstand mental attack.

Ami, however, has fought as long as she can. "I'm going either way," she finally snaps and stalks off with Leal right after her.

"Wait," I cry. "You mustn't run off. It's too danger-ous." But they don't pay any attention. "Oi, come back!"

Elden expels a few words more suited to my uncle's mouth than his. "There's nothing for it, we shall have to go after them. It is sure to be a trap, but at the least we will be together should anything happen. Or, I best say, when something happens." He sighs deeply. Leading this group has no doubt been a much more difficult task than he signed up for. "Come along, then."

It takes some blundering about, but we finally locate the source of the seductive scent: a grove of fragrant apple trees in bloom. To my surprise, the grove is laid out in orderly rows and well-tended. A proper orchard here in the middle of the forest. Several trees already have boughs well-laden with bright, juicy fruit. The thing that really makes me draw in my breath, however, are the blossoms themselves. They are made of dancing fire. Tiny, blazing flowers adorn the boughs and occa-sionally drift off on the wind. It is a sight beautiful enough to make one cry. My own willpower quite gone, I sink down to rest beside the others under one of the blazing trees.

Oh, very well then. But leave the fruit be, at least.

"I never knew something this beautiful could exist," I murmur, then I catch sight of Leal's reaching hand. "No, leave it," I cry out too late.

Ami quickly takes the apple from him and throws it away as hard as she can.

Elden cuffs him on the back of the head. "Leal, you fool! You ought to have learnt by now to leave magic things be."

But the damage is already done.

The air fills with humming. Blossoms are shooting off the trees, though there is not a breeze strong enough to dislodge so much at once. They shift and swirl around us until we stand facing six stately, blazing dryads of the trees. I am surprised to notice two males among them, and terrified to see how heavily armed they are. The women themselves are a sight worthy of dread. They have fierce features to match their fury: sharp jawlines, angular noses, strong arms.

The sight of them alone would be enough to make my knees knock, but it is worse when they speak. They do this in unison: a cold, eerie, echoing chant. "How dare you disturb our peace! Who is it that dares break us? Raid us? Set hand to our sacred fruit? You shall pay." This last word runs with a hollow echo through the wood.

Leal whimpers as he draws his bow.

"Hold," Elden hisses. "You shall not waste those arrows. Think your wood will do them harm?" He turns to the nearest of the dryads. "I do greatly beg your pardon, my lords and ladies. We meant no ill, I assure you. It was only the boy. He is young, hungry, and understood not what he did."

The fiery-petaled sprites are not appeased. In fact,

Elden's speech has only enraged them more. "You shall pay," they cry in a loud voice and begin slowly gliding forward, hemming us in a circle.

"To be sure." Elden speaks boldly, but I hear a quaver in his voice. "I always pay my debts. I have here a fair amount of gold with me."

"You shall pay!"

"Or perhaps you would prefer jewels? I have still this magnificent sword hilt. That is...if you mind not the attached blade, damaged as it is."

"You shall pay!"

"Lord Elden," I squeak, "I think they are asking for much more than gold in payment. They don't exactly have much use for it here."

"Yes, use...useful..." he mutters, then adds in a loud voice, "Or perhaps...perhaps you wish for food in return? A very precious item to us, as we have little to spare. However, we have yet some flop ear left we might part with."

They are not interested in food either.

"YOU SHALL PAY!" And with that last cry, they stretch out blazing hands to grasp us.

The struggle doesn't last long. I land a strike with the new technique Elden taught me but have only a moment of pride before my makeshift dagger incinerates. Hands now empty, I press them both over the dreamsnare where it lies hidden. Partly to protect it, partly hoping I might unlock its secret in time to save us. But I cannot think clearly now. Water, something about water, but there isn't any for miles around.

Leal is trying to throw his bow to safety, but he must throw it through fire and hope it does not catch. Ami and Elden's weapons have grown so hot they are forced to drop them. I can vaguely see Shadegleam prancing and pawing outside the circle, unwilling to abandon his master but unable to help and terrified of the flames.

Within seconds we are all unarmed and held tight in an agonizing furnace. I am losing consciousness. Fast. I clutch the dreamsnare out of desperation and, though I can no longer speak, call out as loud as I can in my thoughts.

Help, Haldis.

But for the first time, she doesn't answer.

Haldis? Do something. Someone. Anyone. If you can hear this, please come. Please help!

And then even my thoughts break. I can only see the fire in front of me, above me, around me. I can feel its heat, forcing my head back and drawing me up to meet it. Just as I lose all hope, I hear a faint tinkling sound.

Hold on.

Haldis! Help.

They are coming. Can you hear them? They are coming. Hold on just a bit longer.

Small black spots cloud my vision, mixing with the red. I am about to faint.

Hold on.

Suddenly, the fire releases me. I drop to the ground, retching. The others are heaped around me, in much the same sad state as myself, but the fire blossom dryads are shrieking and clawing at themselves. Fighting my hazy vision, I make out numerous inkwell spiders crawling about on our attackers, biting and weaving dark webs to trap the fiery limbs. These were the black spots I saw. My friends were not left behind after all. They came to help, just as I asked.

We don't waste time watching. Leal has already scrambled to his bow and is gathering arrows back into his quiver. Ami helps me up while Elden gathers the supplies and weapons we have discarded. And now we are running. Running and running faster than I have ever run before. Running for ages, till my head pounds fit to burst and my legs seize up. I begin tripping on even small objects and eventually crash over a large stone, sprawling onto the pebble-strewn ground. A haze clouds my vision, and all goes black.

❧ 15 ❧

SHATTERING MIRRORS

Shocking cold water drenches my face, and I jerk up, spluttering. The pounding in my head has lessened and the pain in my legs is gone, but with its absence I become aware of a deeper, more insistent pain spearing through me from innumerable places. Glancing down, I find the larger part of my sleeves burned through and my trouser legs now reaching just below the knees. Not to mention singed holes in some very inappropriate places. And I am covered nearly head to foot in bandages. Don't much care to remember how those got there right now. Let's figure out where we are instead.

I raise my head and see a small pond not far away. On my other side lies a large misshapen stone—or more of a small boulder really. It must be what I fell on earlier. There are several more boulders scattered throughout the clearing. Ami is kneeling next to me, a bucket held gingerly in her blistering hands.

"Thank the Powers, you finally woke up!"

"Shouldn't a healer know better than to go dumping buckets of water on people?" I gripe.

"Ah, but my mother was the healer, not me."

"Right. Well, that explains why you do such a terrible job."

"Careful, or I won't redress your burns." She winks. "At least it worked the first time. I would have gotten awfully tired of lugging water over here." She is so encumbered with bandages of her own that I can easily believe it. "And I did try shaking you first. In fact, I was all set on giving up and eating your share of the fish."

"Well, aren't you just the model of friendship." I try to smile and show her I mean it in jest, but my muscles are not very cooperative. "Leave me for dead in a cursed wood just to get an extra portion of pike." I sniff.

She catches on quick. "Oh, but true friendship means not waking the other for something as menial as a bite of fish."

"Is that so?"

"Of course. It's rule number three in the Code of Friendship. And they haven't caught anything near as nice as pike. Mind you, I'm not quite sure what it is, but it's certainly not pike. So, perhaps you won't want any."

"Now, don't go getting too hopeful. I haven't ever had pike before. And neither have you, I'll warrant. We might not have liked it. I'm sure I'll like whatever was caught, and like it much better for being a real cod rather than an imagined pike."

"Oh, well then, I guess I'll have to share." She sighs.

I look around for Elden and Leal. There is no sign of them, other than a decent pile of wood ready for the fire and some fish next to it. I am a bit taken aback by the amount of work they have accomplished and feel guilty for sleeping so long. "There should be plenty of wood here," I muse as Ami starts preparing the fire. "Did they think we needed more?"

"Mm, that's what Lord Elden said. Though I think he just wanted to get Leal aside for a telling off. Didn't want to shame the poor boy more than he had to. They aren't in any better shape than us, though, so they can't be far."

Ami has barely finished speaking when a pleading voice winds its way across the pond. Elden may have meant to be out of earshot, but he has grievously under-estimated the distance Leal's voice can carry.

"I'm ever so sorry, my lord. I didn't mean to. I didn't know—"

"Yet you might well have guessed."

"It was such a nice place. Why should it have been dangerous?"

"And is that not precisely why? It was far too nice a place, which ought to have been a warning."

"I'm sorry, I am. I'll be much more careful in the future. Truly, I will!" Leal is near tears again.

"Well do I know it." Elden's voice softens. He seems satisfied that the boy recognizes the full impact of what he has done. "You made a mistake. It has not been your first, nor shall it be your last. Yet, you must understand the gravity of such a mistake. When you are entrusted with the care of another's life, you cannot take such risks. You *must* learn to be more responsible."

"Yes, my lord."

"Now, come along. We had best get back to the women before something else goes amiss."

"They will be wondering what took so long."

I glance at Ami. "You know, the same could be said to us. It was highly irresponsible asking them to escort us in the first place."

"Now don't you start." She pauses to turn the fish over the fire before continuing, "We did not ask them to come, remember. Elden offered. It was mad to try getting by on our own in here. We would have been dead within days, and he knew it. I expect his conscience wouldn't have let him stay behind even if we had refused his help."

"Still, I'm sure he's regretting it now."

"No, I don't think so. Now, do try not to look so guilty, or they'll know we overheard."

The men are heading back now. Leal racing, eager to get some food, but Elden walks at a much slower pace.

He glances back over his shoulder, pauses to watch us eat for a minute, then veers off into the brush at the side of the pond. Ami isn't looking and Leal hasn't noticed; it's probably nothing important anyway.

"I'm starving," Leal bursts out. "How much of that can I have?"

Ami laughs when I hand him three. "Here, you need to eat well after all that running."

"I do hope we will not be forced to do that again," he groans. "I don't know that I can even walk much for the next few days."

"Me either." Ami sighs. "I don't suppose we'll stay here for a while?"

"I'd rather not." That surprises them; I'm often the first to request a stop. But my legs are feeling better, and it isn't a particularly nice spot. "I am getting dreadfully tired of this wood. I would like to finish my job and get out of it as soon as possible. I suppose even moving slow is better than not at all."

"I don't like this wood much either. It will be nice to head back home." Leal sighs and turns his attention to his meal.

"Home?" Ami hands him her waterskin. "I thought you were going to stay with the dwarves, Leal."

"Ugh, I'd forgotten the dwarves. Never mind, let's stay in here."

Ami chuckles. There must be a story there I have yet to hear.

"But which way do we go now?" I muse. "I wasn't sure where we were before that race, and I'm afraid I lost all direction during it. By the end, I was so far gone, I hardly knew I was running at all. We must be drawing near the desolate side of the wheel, though. I can think of no other reason for such large boulders."

"I don't know, Lady Giselle. But don't you worry, Lord Elden will! And if he does not, he can find out in but a moment."

"How does he do that?" Ami sounds skeptical, but I haven't seen any reason to doubt Elden yet.

"Well," Leal begins, "he will just ask—" He cuts off, looking in the direction Elden disappeared.

I glance up when he stops and notice Elden coming back. There is a man next to him, the same stranger I have seen so many times before. Ah, Elden must ask this man for help! How do they know each other? Seeing them together, I notice the similarities again. Maybe they are kin, after all. Before I can ask Leal, however, the man simply vanishes into thin air.

Elden sits next to me and discreetly slips an arm around my back. "Are you well?" he whispers in my ear.

"Yes," I whisper back. "Are you?"

"Of course." He smiles reassuringly, but no amount of kind words or cheerful smiles can cover his haggard appearance or the worry in his eyes.

"What's wrong?"

He shakes his head, in answer or warning I'm not

TO SLAY A CURSE

sure, and takes his share of the fish. I think it best to let him eat in silence and turn back to my own meal.

Finally, Ami speaks up. "I don't want to disturb you, Lord Elden, but we were discussing which would be the best direction to go. Leal assured us you would know."

"Are you that eager to continue at once? You would not rather rest a while longer?"

She gives me a pointed look, and his bewildered gaze follows. But seeing his exhaustion, I don't have the heart to ask him to move again today. "It's nothing," I shrug, "we could all use a bit more rest."

"But you just said you wanted to escape the wood as soon as possible and moving slowly is better than not at all."

I groan. Thank you, Leal.

Elden's eyes soften. "Is that truly what you would like?"

"No."

"Yes," Ami counters.

I shoot her a harsh glance then shake my head. "It's fine. One day won't make much difference. You obviously need the break."

"Don't worry about me."

Ami snorts, but all his attention is focused on me. "Giselle," he takes me by the shoulders, "this is a simple question. Do you want to leave now? Yes or no?"

The others have already answered for me, and at this point, I'm not sure he will accept another.

Answer truthfully, child. No one will hold it against you.

"Yes," I sigh.

He smiles and claps me on the arm. "Then we shall leave now." Turning to Ami, he adds, "I do, in fact, know which direction to go."

"See, I told you," Leal crows.

She shakes her head. "But how do—"

"Leave it!" I cut her off. Though I'm just as curious, now is not the time.

We tarry just long enough for Ami to check over our wounds. The burns are still quite nasty, but with a new application of salve, I don't notice the pain that much. The older wounds have healed exceedingly quick. In fact, my injuries from the jeweled beasts are all but gone. I'll take that as a good omen. We have caught our breath; now it is time to finish the race.

❦

IN THE RUSH TO FINISH EATING AND PACK, I DID NOT get the chance to bring the topic of the stranger up. And, once the packing was done, Elden set such a quick pace that talk became nearly impossible.

So now, several agonizing hours later, I can only speculate answers to the questions chasing their tails through my head. *Who* is that man, and *why* does he keep appearing at the most unlikely times? My heart, at least, says he is helping, but my mind is not so sure. Why does he never speak to anyone? Why does he vanish every time I try to get a good look at him? What does he want?

I find no answers, but the guessing keeps my mind occupied and off the ache working its way through my very bones. Not that I have a right to complain after forcing everyone to march today. So, I keep my mouth shut and trudge on with head bowed. But at long last, it is growing dark.

Elden has begun slowing the pace. Then stops all together when Leal, who of course still has energy to spare, offers to scout ahead. I drop to the ground, gasping heavily, and pull out my dreamsnare. A squeak escapes my breathless lungs. Over half gone now. And not much that can be done about it. Though that doesn't stop me shaking the thing, furiously. As if I can frighten it into turning back of its own accord. But alas, no such luck. Sighing, I tuck it back in my tunic before Elden notices. No sense adding to his burdens.

No sooner have I hidden the talisman than Leal's pounding feet arrive. "I have found the most perfect place to make camp, my lord. It's just over there through the trees. There is a cleared area and a tall bowed over cliff with a sort of hollowed-out spot at the base. You can see the top from here." He points out a rather daunting crag peeking above the treetops. It is large enough that I'm surprised I didn't notice it before. "It is almost a proper cave," he continues, "and very secure.

We can shelter in there and not have to worry about watching our backs."

Elden claps the proud boy on the shoulder. "Well done! I could do without guard duty tonight. What do you think?"

"True," the boy replies. "I could even do without food if it means I get to sleep the night through."

Elden laughs. "I doubt it shall come to that. Though you are not likely to get as much as you wish. We shall all have to tighten our belts from here on out. The land is growing sparse and our supplies are dangerously low."

Within half an hour, we have arrived at the cliff and built a small fire, mostly for comfort rather than protection. It is a cozy spot, really. Much cooler and less stuffy than anywhere else we have stayed the night in this wood. It is not till I lay down and am half asleep that the stranger returns to my mind. I groan. I'm far too tired for questions tonight and Elden is very likely asleep already. Tomorrow. I *will* find out tomorrow.

A SLIGHT PRESSURE ON MY SHOULDER WAKES ME. THE first thing I notice is a complete absence of pain, as if Ami has applied a double-strength salve to my burns. Struggling to pry my eyes open, I find a tall figure looming over me. I scuffle back, heart in my throat—only to end up pressed against the rough wall, casting about me for anything of use. But there is no escape. And Elden is still rolled in his blanket, sleeping soundly. How could we have assumed this place was safe? We should have set a guard!

But the man makes no further move toward me. And that's when I realize he was not facing me at all. He moves away and my breath comes easier.

Until he kneels by Ami. I bolt up, trying to scream a warning and only succeeding in a strangled squeal before choking off. The intruder is the only one to react, the others too deeply wrapped in slumber, and he turns back to me. As he does, the embers' glow lights his face. It is the pale-robed stranger who has entered our camp.

My heart abandons my throat in favor of breaking right through my ribcage. Why has he come now? What does he want?

It's okay. He means you no harm.

I know Haldis would not lie to me. But my body takes longer to accept this fact than my mind. I stand before him trembling, trying desperately to calm my erratic breathing and still the anxious tears trickling from my eyes.

"There is nothing to fear, my child," he soothes as he presses me to lie back down, not ungently.

"Who are you?" Though my voice is barely audible, its quavering is pronounced. "Why have you been following me?"

He smiles slightly. "Do you not know? Then you soon

will. But for now, you must sleep." He puts a light hand on my forehead and my eyes drift closed of their own accord.

I OPEN MY EYES TO THE DAWN, FEELING AS IF THERE IS something I ought to remember. A cursory search of my surroundings yields no answers. Just Ami and Elden standing a bit apart from the campsite, looking through supplies. They are probably deciding if we must skip breakfast today. Leal still lies tightly wrapped in his cloak.

Getting up, I notice that I have no pain. I gasp and look down. My tunic and trousers have been repaired, good as new. I pull up my sleeves to find myself bandage-free and the burns completely healed. There must be some magic in this place.

"Ami," I call as I run out to show her. "Ami, my burns."

"I know." Her clothes have also been repaired. "Mine are healed and so are Lord Elden's. And look here." She opens a pack I have never seen. I look and find it full of fish, cured meat, and even bread.

"I just don't understand how it happened," she continues. "I have never known a burn that healed this fast, and I know we did not miss an entire bag of food when we took stock."

"No, we did not overlook it," Elden assures her with a fond grin. "It was given to us."

"What? Who could possibly have done that?"

"It was him," I gasp. Memory suddenly flowing through me. "It must have been him. He was here last night. Scared me half to death."

"Who is that, Giselle?" Ami screws her mouth up, perturbed.

I suppose I'm not making sense. "The pale stranger."

"I'm sorry, who?" She looks at me like I've lost my mind.

"The strange man dressed in pale robes. Haven't you seen him? He's been following us since we came into the wood. He fought the scary man in black robes and brought Shadegleam back when we left the river." I turn to Elden. "I know you have seen him, Lord Elden. You were talking with him just yesterday. Who is he?"

"Yes, I know him well. He is a dear friend," he replies with a wide smile.

"Pale stranger!" A laugh comes from behind me. We have woken Leal. "You have been calling him that? You do not know who he is, Lady Giselle?"

"No, I do not," I reply a bit defensively. Honestly, how could the boy have expected me to know someone I've never been introduced to! "I know he has been following us. I sometimes think he means to help. And I have only now become aware he is a friend of your master's. But that is all."

"Gosh, you should have asked before! I can tell you all about him. He is—"

A loud screech and blinding light drown out the explanation I have been waiting so long to hear.

Perched above us on the clifftop is an enormous bird. A hawk, I think, at least half as big as Shadegleam. It shines so bright; I have trouble seeing it well. I squint, trying to make out exactly what this new threat is, and then understand why. The hawk is made up of hundreds, possibly thousands, of tiny mirrors, each one reflecting the newly risen sun.

"Aww, blast!" Leal cries.

We all press as close to the cliff as possible.

"Back to the hollow!" Elden instructs, just as the hawk launches into the air. Luckily, it is too large and heavy to change course quickly and has some trouble getting around the large overhang and close enough to the cliff face to reach us. But that won't save us for long.

I stumble against something, a small rock. Without thinking I pick it up and hurl it at the massive hawk. I don't expect much. Nothing helped against the wolves or the dryads. But this time, my weapon deals some damage. The bird takes a solid hit to the wing, shattering a few mirrors. It screeches and begins wobbling as it flies. The others have reached the hollow already.

"Hit it," I call. "Rocks, heavy sticks, anything." I am almost there now. But even the hollow isn't small enough to keep the bird out, and hiding there will most likely result in a trap. But we don't have much choice.

Leal is trying to string his bow, his hands shaking so much he drops it. Elden has a few of the logs remaining from last night's fire. Just as I dive into the relative safety of our camp, he throws. The hit lands so hard the hawk drops to the ground, shards of glass scattering everywhere.

For a minute, I am irrationally disappointed. That was almost too easy, considering the difficulty we had with our other assailants. But I thought too soon. The beast shakes its head with an earsplitting screech and struggles to its feet. A few lurching steps of crunching gravel and glass. Moments later the bird takes wing again, and we have nowhere else to go.

Ami is throwing the few pebbles she can find, along with a fair amount of our baggage, but it's not doing much good. A slight breeze grazes my face as an arrow whizzes past me, but it doesn't make a direct hit, glancing to the side.

What we really need is to trap the bird. Breaking the mirrors injures it, but not enough. And there are too many mirrors to smash all of them. The hawk is nearly on top of us now, still flying under the overhang.

The overhang! If I can use it just right...

I feel my dreamsnare heating up fast, faster than it ever has before.

"Everyone out. Get out of the hollow on the far side. Now!"

A mad scramble. The rock above us is beginning to shake and crack. I don't have much control once it starts to go and put on a burst of speed. Thankfully, everyone else is already out. I have just made it over the edge when the entire cliff face surrounding the hollow falls, crushing the bird completely. Not a single mirror left intact.

Elden catches me as I fall to my knees, gasping. He wraps me protectively in his arms and my breathing gradually slows to match his. I look over his shoulder at the wreckage. We lost the hawk. We also, however, lost quite a few useful things. Such as bed rolls. Still, we made it out and, thanks to Ami, so did most of our baggage.

Leal is gaping at the destruction, a frantic look in his eyes. "He is growing more powerful."

"No, not as bad as that. Only more desperate, I think," Elden responds calmly. "I would wager that was a final attempt to distract us. A bit obvious really, and he was nearly too late."

"What are you talking about?"

"Is it this stranger of Giselle's?" Ami huffs. "Is he the one that sent that monster? How can you be certain he means well?"

"Of course, it wasn't him," Leal snaps. "It was that no-good wizard!"

"Peace, Leal. Keep in mind they have not the same understanding as us. There is much to explain." Elden releases me to stand at arm's length, making it easier to address both Ami and myself. "What Leal was about to tell you before he was so disturbingly interrupted, Lady Giselle, is that the man you have been referring to as the pale stranger is, in fact, the Creative One himself. And that," he indicates the heap of rubble with a wave of his arm, "was done at the Dark Power's bidding. It is the work of the wizard Rajani."

16

RACING THE WIND

"No," Ami gasps. "No, it can't be Rajani. I mean, he was banished years ago!"

"That would hardly stop him," Elden replies, "and who would come in the wood to check?"

This makes no sense. Rajani is a wizard in *my* world. But then, so is Ami. Not a wizard, of course, but a very real, very alive person in both worlds. Now that I know even Eamon and Gil have counterparts here, I should not be so surprised to find that he has one too. Especially considering the villainous role he's played in my life. I just never considered it. I saw him here once, casting the curse in that shadowed lane, but it was only a memory. Has he really been with us the whole time? Why wouldn't he have shown himself? We could hardly be a proper threat to him. Surely, he could have come and finished us off the first night we camped beneath the trees. Although, he may have shown himself and I just didn't realize.

Confirmation hits hard enough to knock the wind from me as an image flashes through my mind. Another memory, though not shadowed: a dark figure being dragged away by a pale one.

"Wait, I have seen him too. The stranger—I mean the Creative One—was fighting him after that night in the dell. When we were all arguing about where to go. I saw them both." Odd that I have seen the stranger many times but not noticed Rajani once since then. I do remember a foreboding sense, the vague knowledge that danger followed us, but I have not felt even that in quite a long time. Perhaps trying to solve the puzzle of the stranger kept my mind too distracted.

"That would not be considered such a strange sight," Elden replies gravely. "The two Powers have been at war since man first woke upon the sacred plain. Or, more to the purpose, the Dark Power has waged war upon the Creative One."

"For hundreds and thousands of years," Leal chimes in. "He just keeps going and keeps going. Because he is so full of the Darkness itself, he can't do anything else anymore. That's why the Ivory Isle calls on Ivlin for help." He looks down and continues in a very un-Leal-like whisper, "Sometimes, I am afraid we might lose."

Ami puts a hand on his shoulder. "That is nothing to be ashamed of, Leal. Everyone has doubts."

"Not about something like this. Not something so important," he mutters.

This is the first time I've seen him genuinely downcast. The boy is so overconfident about everything that experiencing a dose of doubt might just do him some good.

"Especially in matters of importance such as this," Elden corrects him. Adding encouragingly, "I have doubted from time to time, myself. Our strength comes not in lack of fear, but in the ability to set those doubts aside and continue fighting. More important still, remember who is fighting for us."

Fighting for us. A nice thought. But where do they come into it? "Are you part of the war?"

The incredulous look Elden turns to me has me backtracking fast as a wink. "Wait, that didn't come out right. Obviously, being a knight, you are required to be on the front lines. It's just that I thought you were given a post with the dwarves."

"This is no common war. Think of all the centuries that have passed. When a war is fought this long, there are always other matters that must be attended to. And naturally, alliances must be maintained."

"What started the war?"

"Pride and envy. A simple answer, it would seem, yet there is much that lurks behind it and may take a while in the telling."

"Then tell us as we walk," Ami cuts him off. "We

don't want to hang around here too long and risk being attacked again." She eyes the fallen cliff warily.

"At least the cliff is a good sign," I say as I check how much time my trick bought us. It isn't nearly as much as I had hoped. Half a small strand at the most. But I force my brow to remain clear and my tone light. "Rockier terrain, which will hopefully mean less underbrush and easier walking."

"More importantly, it ought to mean getting closer to the monster's lair," Ami adds. "If we are right about it living in a sparse, rocky place."

"A place you didn't think possible to be found in this wood. Did you, Lady Ami?" Leal teases.

Ami pulls a face. "Sometimes, Leal, it is a good thing to be proven wrong. Just as it is often better to hold your tongue. A trick you have yet to learn. Now, go see about calming the horse down or we will be carrying all of this ourselves."

I thought the way would be easier, now that we don't have the thickets and drooping tree limbs to contend with, but climbing around or over what is left of the cliff turns out to be just as hard.

As we stumble and slip on the slabs of stone, Elden starts his explanation over. "The Great War was brought on due to an overabundance of envy and pride. The Dark Power had once another name, though none now remember it. For in that time, he was a close friend of the Creative One, his most trusted servant, it is said. As age followed age, he had watched and marveled at all the wonderful things the Creative One made. Yet when he attempted the feat himself, he found that he had not this skill. Soon, growing envious of the Creative One's ability, he determined to become greater. The greatest of all powers. This pride led him to search out and consume the Darkness.

"He spent well-nigh a century in learning its ways, and he did indeed grow powerful. With this power, he could now create things of his own. Yet, they were imitations only, marred aberrations of the Creative One's own works. Seeing this, he became enraged. Accusing the Creative One of trickery, he vowed revenge. Yet without enough power to attack the Creative One directly, he has resorted to doing away with the creation."

"But, if so, shouldn't the world be forsaken, barren, or burning all down to ash?" I didn't mean to ponder it aloud, but Elden just smiles.

"Nay, he does not destroy completely." He pauses to catch me by the elbow as I tip backwards from an unsteady rock and keeps a light hold as we continue, matching his pace to mine.

"Well, go on then," I huff, breathless with exertion. "How does he destroy?"

"Kill someone and they can no longer suffer, tear something down and it can be rebuilt. Rather, the Dark Power has become a master of deception, distraction. The wilds are now places of fear. Only on the Ivory Isle do man and beast truly live in companionship. And man himself is oppressed most of all. What the Creative One took the most care to form, pouring out a large part of himself in the molding, is made to forget his maker and believe himself worthless, distracted by the deceptive beauty of the Dark Power's creations."

"Or living miserable half-lives under the power of his curses, which have been his greatest weapons," Ami speaks for the first time.

I didn't realize she knew this story as well. Must I always be the last one in everything? "And that is why he has been attacking us? Or, sending Rajani to do so? To distract me and keep me from breaking the curse. All those monsters were his creations?"

"Yes."

"Then he really is too powerful."

"No, Lord Elden is right," Leal calls from ahead, posing atop a large boulder like a hero of old. "He can't win. Not even when he thinks he has. The Creative One is much more powerful."

And for the rest of the day, as the trees continue to thin and the terrain becomes steeper, Leal regales us with stories of the Dark Power's numerous failures.

I AM WHEEZING AS I REACH THE TOP OF A NARROW plateau nestled between the outcropping rock and widening to a stone-strewn expanse behind it. We are in the foothills of the mountains now. So close to the end of this ordeal. So close to freedom. But then, I have been learning a lot about the Creative One these past few days. I am beginning to think that with him, I can live a happy life regardless, even while under the curse. Though I'm still going to try to set myself free, of course. I know now that he wants me free even more than I do.

Elden calls a rest and I turn back a moment, hand shading my eyes from the slanting sun, to survey our day's accomplishment. But the sight that meets my eyes rips a scream from my throat. A veritable army pursues us from out of the wood. An army that was certainly not there when I glanced back a half hour ago.

I count at least eight gem wolves racing full speed toward us. A storm of fire blossoms swirl in their wake. Three of the giant hawks are soaring far above them, mirrors glinting in the sunlight. But worst of all is the tall man in the dark cloak running in their midst.

"Giselle, get down!" I don't move quickly enough, and Ami tackles me to the ground. Then seizing my arm, she jerks me behind a boulder and crouches low over me, the sharp rock lacerating us both. She looks down at me with tears in her eyes. "I think you will have to go on without us now."

"What are you talking about? We must run faster."

"No, Giselle," Elden counters. "You must leave us."

"But why?"

"We have but one horse," Ami reminds me. "We cannot all outrun what is coming. But you can get away if we buy you time."

My throat tightens and my chest aches. I can't speak but frantically shake my head.

"Leal shall accompany you," Elden decides quickly. "You will not be alone. But you must make haste."

The boy nods and begins removing packs from Shadegleam's back.

I finally manage to force out a word. "No."

I cautiously glance around the boulder. There are so many of them, and they are closing the distance faster than ought to be physically possible. What we took a day to cover... well, we have not got much time. "I can't." My hands are trembling slightly. "I can't just leave you alone to face...*that*."

"Giselle," Ami pleads, "it is all about distraction, remember? This is just another distraction."

"And you mustn't allow him to waylay you again," Elden argues. "You are too near the goal for that."

"But I count fifteen at least! Fifteen against two? And one a wizard with the Dark Power's aide. You will never make it out." It is not just my hands shaking now.

"But we aren't the ones who need to make it out, are we?" Ami asks gently. If she is trying to soothe me, she is going about it the wrong way.

"And I would not be so quick to give us up for dead,"

Elden adds. "We have the high ground, and the passage is quite narrow here. They shall have to come through only a few at a time. We may make it out yet. If not, it is our duty to see you get out safely. By the time we fall, you will be far out of range."

"How could you ask me to do this? I can't. I won't!"

"You haven't got a choice, Giselle!"

"You must go and go swiftly."

"There are still the birds, of course." Leal speaks for the first time, finishing his work. "But I am confident we will outrun them."

The din of vicious howling fills the air, and I glance up to see the hawks are no more than a bowshot away. If we are going, it must be now or not at all.

"It's all right, Lady Giselle." Leal turns to me, holding out his hand. "Come on."

Despairing I take it and feel him shaking as well. His eyes betray his fear, but his jaw is determinedly set as he helps me mount. Quickly swinging up in front of me, he gathers the reins. "I'll look after her, master, don't worry. Hold tight, Lady Giselle."

Shadegleam surges forward with the force of a gale, just as the foremost of the screeching hawks arrives.

I take one last glance back at my friends and could swear there is a flash of white light. But then we round a boulder and I lose them. In fact, I don't see much but Leal's rough cloak and the blunt edges of rocks, looming up and receding as we pass, in what has become a very treacherous race. I mustn't hope for too much; the light was likely a reflection off one of the birds—an easy deduction to make as we bend low to avoid the grasping talons behind us.

But it may not have been. He could have come.

I screech as loud as the pursuing hawks when a hard wing clips the side of my head and sharp claws rake across my back. But I don't dare let go of Leal to fend them off. He coaxes Shadegleam to a further feat of speed, and we pull slightly ahead of the menace again. Just when we have gained a short lead, however, the ground drops out from under us. Everything suddenly becomes a swirl of color, confusion, and pain as we tumble down.

17

ON OUR OWN

Gasping and hacking, a sharp pain in my side, I look up through the haze of dust raised by our descent to see a jumble of boulders strewn with broken glass. One last hawk looses a furious screech as it wings a hasty yet unsteady retreat. My vision blurs as I watch it go and I blink furiously, trying to focus on my immediate surroundings. When it clears, I find I'm sprawled on my back at the bottom of a steep gorge. It is quite narrow, with roughhewn, biting edges, and there is absolutely no way back up. My breath hitches as I swallow a sob. Blinking away the creeping tears, I force myself to take deep breaths through the pain and consider the positive. We can't go back, but no enemy can pursue us.

Leal starts to stir and moans slightly. I crawl over to him. "Leal! Leal, are you all right?"

He sits up hesitantly. "I...I think so." He looks around, bleary-eyed, and then focuses on my face. "Oh, Lady Giselle!" His eyes grow large as saucers and full of tears. "Lady, your head."

I can feel the warm, sticky blood matting my hair and trickling down my cheek. Add this to all the cuts, bruises, and potentially cracked ribs and I'm sure I look a fright. But then, he looks one too. "Oh, it's nothing." I wave him away. "I promise it looks worse than it is. I can clean up later. But are you sure you are all right? No trouble breathing? No broken bones?"

He checks himself over. "No," he finally replies. "No, I'm fine." He glances to the side and lets loose a guttural, earsplitting scream, his face crumpled and eyes bulging. "No. Oh, no, no, no. Warmund!"

Warmund?

The horse.

Oh, yes. I had forgotten that was Shadegleam's real name.

Leal scrambles over the rocks, slipping several times in his haste, to where the horse lies, its foam-flecked sides heaving.

"Warmund, my poor friend."

At the sound of his voice, the distraught animal begins snorting heavily, screaming, and thrashing about as it attempts to rise.

"Easy. Easy now. That's a good boy," Leal soothes, running a hand over the horse's neck, the other resting on its muzzle. Shadegleam tosses his head a few more times and then lies still.

I help Leal remove the rest of the baggage strapped to the frightened animal. Not a significant feat as we are down to just our own two. Continuing to speak quietly, reassuring Shadegleam there is nothing to fear, Leal carefully runs his hands over every inch of the froth-flecked coat, from ears straight down to hooves. "A miracle," he breathes. "Not a single break. You are going to be just fine."

While Leal stays with the horse, I wash off the blood smeared over my face and try to fix up the gash. I am reluctant to use what little drinking water we have left, but I know not cleaning the wound out properly will only get me killed with an infection. So, I grit my teeth and pour as slowly as possible, hoping to save as much water as I can. I can tell the gash is not too deep as I wrap a cloth several times around my head and turn to my side, which is throbbing as bad as ever. Removing my belt and gently pulling the tunic away, I see a large, dark bruise the size of my fist. It looks like I have broken one, if not two, ribs. Not much can be done about it now, though. So I bind it as tightly as possible and sit down, contemplating never moving again.

Once Leal has cleaned himself up—no terribly serious injuries there either, thank the Powers—he coaxes Shadegleam back on his hooves. A groan slips past my lips as I force myself to stand and shoulder a bag, which Leal quickly takes from me.

"Well, best be getting on then," he declares with a hopeful look back the way we came. But even the ever-optimistic Leal can see the only way to go is forward. So, with a small shrug, he leads our stumbling way further into the gorge.

It gets dark much earlier down here; the tall walls block the setting sun. I draw my badly torn shawl closer around me as we near the end of the gorge. Another wall blocks us in. Leal drops to his knees and I follow suit. But I'm not as devastated as I ought to be, seeing it all end here. Instead, I'm just grateful for the excuse to lie down. It's painful enough to breathe, much less walk.

Leal, however, is not taking it well. I wrap an arm around the sniffling boy. "Let's sleep the night through. We can find a way out in the morning."

He nods and forces a smile. "We are not giving up yet."

"No. Not giving up, just resting. The morning will bring new hope."

I wrap him in my arms, excusing it as a need for extra warmth, and the exhausted boy is out like a dampened candle. I lie there, listening to his steady breathing and desperately trying to imagine my way out of this. Anything I could use my talisman for to save us from starving to death in this living tomb. But no spark of inspiration comes to me. My mind only buzzes with the horrific events of the day. Envisioning my friends' deaths over and over. When I can't take it anymore, I force my eyes shut. I told Leal to sleep and find hope in the morning. It's time I took my own advice. Attuning my breaths to his, I eventually drift off.

Hope does indeed come with the morning. I rise early to inspect our dead end and the pale light reveals a small passage. It's gouged deep in the far corner and partially obscured by a heap of boulders, but it looks just big enough to get the horse through. I slip in and make sure we can get all the way through before waking Leal. It's narrow, and I emerge with a good number of scrapes I didn't have before, but we can all make it.

☙❧

I TRUDGE THE BARREN ASCENT WITH HUNCHED shoulders, huddling deeper into my shawl as I fight to pull it tight against the biting wind. I laugh through chattering teeth when I think of how desperate I was for air not so long ago. I would give almost anything to take back the old terrain—stuffy, green, and hot—now that I'm left with only bleak, sharp, and cold.

"I think it's your turn now, Lady Giselle." Leal hands me his cloak. We've lost even our last blanket now to the sporadically shifting rock and have only his cloak and my shawl to keep warm. Leal has been insisting we share the cloak and won't listen when I claim the shawl is enough. But this time, I don't have the heart to take it. The boy's lips are chapped to bleeding. His hands remain blue no matter how often I rub them.

"I can manage. You keep it for a while."

"Then how about a short rest? We don't have to be in such an awful hurry now. There hasn't been anyone following us for days." He doesn't say it, but I know he isn't just thinking about the enemy. If our friends were going to catch up, they would have done it by now. We haven't been covering that much ground with our injuries. Every day we are alone, I can see the hope dim in the soul-weary boy's eyes.

"That's a very sensible idea, Leal." I drop the packs and let them lay where they fall. "We will camp here for the night, then. I know there's not much left to work with, but I'll make your favorite stew for dinner."

"No need, lady. You ought to stay still as much as possible. Those cracked ribs are far from healed yet. I can fetch us something."

I subconsciously put a hand to my side as he helps me sit with my back against Shadegleam's warm flank. My head wound is progressing rather well, but he's right about this. We have done nothing but climb up this mountain ever since finding a way out of the gorge. Something my aching ribs do not thank me for. Every breath I draw is a dagger in my side. I'm starting to worry they won't ever heal properly with all this exertion, but there's nothing else I can do.

Leal manages to coax a fitful fire from the sparse kindling available. He prepares the meager meal, and we eat in silence. There is never laughter around our fires anymore, nor the tinkling of my inky friends. I can't even remember the last time Leal told me a story. Sometime that first day out from the gorge, I think. When he comes to sit next to me, I spread the ragged cloak over us and hold him close. He snuggles against me and finally starts to warm up. I don't think he'll stay conscious long enough for guard duty.

He always insists on taking first watch, of course, and often won't wake me for my turn at all. Whenever I suggest doing away with the practice altogether, he panics. "What if they are still looking for us? They might catch us again. Someone has to be alert." But tonight, he hasn't even considered it. The boy with the unquenchable spirit has finally given up.

His eyes are closed, and his breathing has evened out, but I don't think he's quite asleep yet. "Thank you, Leal," I murmur in his ear. "You are taking such good care of me. Lord Elden would be proud." His hand tightens on my arm briefly. I have finally drawn it out: his smile. The ghost of a mischievous grin that once came as easily as breathing. Then he drifts off.

I compulsively check my dreamsnare—not that I

need the added misery as I watch the darkness slowly claw its way up the last fourth of my talisman.

I sigh and stare up at the stars. One of the few awe-inspiring sights in this desolation. By the Powers, we desperately need something to cheer us up.

⚘

IT IS A RARE DAY OF BRIGHT SUNSHINE, WARMING BOTH the air and the despair hanging over us. We have finally reached the far side of the mountain and come across the first bit of vegetation we have seen in days. Scraggly bushes and stunted trees, gradually gathering into a denser thicket. I smile and reach out to touch the trees, pricking my finger on thorns. Still, it is so nice to see anything aside from rocks for a change. I can hear a pounding sound coming from somewhere close.

"Oh, come have a look at this, Lady Giselle!"

I hurry to join Leal. There is a river below us, flowing swiftly from the power of a large waterfall further upstream, sending spray several feet into the air.

"Isn't it wonderful?" His eyes are sparkling and a grin larger than I've seen in weeks covers his face.

"Yes, it is very beautiful. And I am so thankful for a chance to wash some of this grime off."

"And refill our waterskins. I'm tired of living off muddy puddles."

"Quite right! Are you ready to go down?"

"Race you!" He laughs and takes off, whooping as he sprints down the bank and into the water.

I follow more slowly, not losing my head enough to risk my neck on the descent. When I make it down, he helps me fill the waterskins and then climbs out to give Shadegleam a rub down. "You'll enjoy this, my friend. Haven't had anything nice in a long time, have you?"

I leave him to it and take a dip myself. The water is cool but not as cold as the snowmelt I expected. Refreshing. I can feel the dirt, worry, and pain of the past washing off. I swim about a bit, trying to make my way further upstream, but the current is too strong. Sighing, I let myself drift back to shore and find Leal sprawled out on the rocks, fast asleep. Not feeling at all tired myself, I take a walk up the bank, letting the sun dry me.

Once I'm near the waterfall, I can see a sort of ledge making a pathway around the cliff behind it. That doesn't look natural. I wonder how it got there. After a few minutes, my curiosity gets the better of me, and I go to investigate.

The ledge starts just where the riverbank meets the rocky precipice from which the water pours out into the river. It is only wide enough for one person to walk at a time, and the wall behind it is covered in strange mark-ings, symbols skillfully carved into the uneven rock.

I turn and shout to Leal, "Come here." There is no response. "Leal," I try again, "get up. Come look at this."

But he cannot hear me over the roaring water. Poor boy, he deserves a good sleep anyway. I'll just take a quick look around and be back before he wakes up. I walk quickly along the ledge, behind the water, and into what appears to be a tunnel.

There are more markings here that I cannot read, but this time they are paired with pictures. I am surprised to see an inkwell spider among the creatures depicted on the wall.

It quickly grows too dim to see the carvings clearly. But then I notice a few lit torches in brackets on the wall further ahead. Someone must live here. Perhaps I should go back. But the pictures are so captivating. They appear to be telling a story, one I would like to finish.

Just a bit further. This is important.

Reassured by Haldis' insistence, I continue. The further I go, the more I seem to recognize images in the carvings. Many of them are detailed representations of the stories Elden and Leal have told me about the Creative One and this Great War.

Spellbound, I walk on and on, with no notion of passing time or how far I have come. That is, until I trip, and my torch goes out. "Blast!" My shout echoes back to me, bouncing off the walls in an eerie cry. Suddenly, I notice how exhausted and ravenous I am. My side is aching again. I had better get back. I've spent much longer here than I meant to. Leal must be worried sick.

I turn and hurry back along the passage, retracing

my steps, a hand along the wall to keep me from falling or getting lost in a side passage.

❧

I HAVE BEEN WORKING BACKWARDS FOR WHAT FEELS like hours now. I'm beginning to get frightened. What if I can't find my way out? I must have come in much deeper than I thought. It can't possibly have taken me this long before. Oh, why wasn't I sensible enough to wait for Leal? He would have liked to see the paintings. This one mistake trumps every impulsive, outlandish thing that rash boy has done since we met. How long ago was that now? A month? Two months? I can't remember anymore. I can't think here, alone in the dark.

The black is pressing on my eyes, my hands, my mind. My feet are beginning to drag. My stomach has gone from grumbling to roaring for food. I'm never going to make it out. I am going to die of starvation here in the dark, and Leal will never know what happened. He will be all alone. Worse, he will come looking for me, then get himself lost and die alone in the dark too.

No, he won't. Keep going. You are almost there.

But time passes, and I still can't locate the entrance. I am just about to sit down and cry when I hear something. A distant rumble. Stumbling as I speed up, I see a faint light illuminating a wide hole with water falling over it. Yes! I've made it after all.

There now. Didn't I tell you?

But when I arrive at the opening, I realize this can't possibly be the same waterfall I came in through. The light is all wrong. It should be night by now, anyway. And the water itself is incredible. It is glowing a myriad of colors. A rainbow woven in mist. And there, in a lush glade behind it, stands the blurred figure of a man.

18

BEHIND THE MAGIC VEIL

The man motions for me to join him. I can't stay in this tunnel forever, and it's clear I won't be finding my way back to the riverside. I take a deep breath and step through the falls, emerging perfectly dry on the other side. Puzzled, I look back. The water still falls hard and fast. The jeweled mist still wafts up to the azure sky. But not a drop splashes the ground beneath. Nor does the cascade roar in my ears. In fact, the only thing I can hear is a muted tinkling about my ankles.

If my guard wasn't up already, it is now. The glade is steeped in magic. It strongly reminds me of my last encounter with a magical clearing. I won't survive another ordeal of that sort. Not on my own. This glade, however, has a different feel—magical, yes, but more wholesome. The colors are not as bright or fair but much richer, deeper than anything I have ever seen. As if more real or alive than even my own world.

A surprisingly fresh scent does permeate the air, yet it is not intoxicating. My mind does not become muddled as it did in the apple orchard. Nor is there a single blazing petal in sight. In their place, winking lights drift amidst the grasses. A winking I am quite familiar with—that of light glancing off a crystalline body as it weaves an inky web.

"Be not afraid."

I turn to the man at last and he stretches out his hand. No, I am no longer afraid. And yet, I hesitate.

"Child, do you still not know me?"

I know him. Of course, I do. I hadn't needed to see his face to know he is my stranger. This new magic, the inkwell spiders, my complete ease—all tell me as much. But now that I do look at him, I am not sure what to do.

"You are the Creative One, Lord." I perform an awkward curtsy.

"Stand, stand! No need for ceremony here. You have done well, child. Come now, I have a meal prepared."

I can see no evidence of a meal, but I tentatively reach out my hand and place it in his.

He leads me to a small table that springs up from the ground at his command, fashioned from a felled oak and beautifully carved. He has but to touch the table and a feast appears. I sit cautiously on one of the chairs, half afraid it will sink back into the moss. When I find that it holds my weight, I relax, settling back and reaching for a warm honey roll. But I drop my hand halfway there when a realization hits me. This is a reward I have not earned.

Shame washes over me. I have no right to eat this. I do not deserve so much kindness after all the selfish things I have done. I deserted my friends to save my own life. They are *dead*. I let them *die* in my place. Worse, I abandoned Leal. I left a small, sleeping boy alone in the wild to look at carven images. He will be awake by now, only to find me gone. And he will blame himself. I had not even the decency to ask after my only friends in this world now that there is someone here who could tell me. I bow my head, unable to look at the Creative One or his bounty. What must he think of me now?

"You need not fear for the boy, dear one. Nor grieve for your friends." He hands me the largest honey roll on the platter.

"You mean, they are alive? They aren't dead?" I can hardly believe it. Leal held on to that hope much longer than I did.

"Dead? No, I do not abandon my own so easily."

I flinch, though his words are kind. It was far too easy for me. I ought to have argued more. Simply put my foot down and refused to go.

He lifts my chin with a gentle finger, meeting my eyes with a kindly gaze. "They live and are yet well. The young Leal woke to find his master by his side."

"This...oh...this is so wonderful! Can I see them? They will be worried about me. I've been gone so long."

"It has not been as long there. I spoke to them by the falls. You are now under my care. Elden leads the rest to Ivlin as we speak."

"The rest? Ami is going, too? And what of the dwarves?"

"Yes, Amita does not return to her bondage. She goes to train for the Ivlin Blades. Lord Elden will see her safely there and then take up his post. Your friends are safe and at peace. Nor are you to blame for any of the danger they have faced."

His kind eyes and bright smile are so familiar. I am struck again by the resemblance he bears to Lord Elden —or that Lord Elden bears to him. I have even seen Eamon wear this same look on several occasions. "My Lord—Creative One?"

"Yes, dear one. What is it you would ask?"

"I was only wondering, why does Lord Elden look like you? Are you kin?"

"Kin." He hums. "You are quite observant. Yes, we are kin in a way. For he too is my child, my dear one. And your Eamon as well, though younger to my reckoning. All who enter into my service become my children. The more they heed me, the longer they serve, the more like me they become. You may find this true of yourself in time."

"Oh."

I'm not quite sure how to follow up an odd comment like that, so I begin eating again. Silence spreads between us. Not an awkward silence like you would expect with most great Lords and Powers, but an easy companionable silence that encourages thought. I think back over all the times I have seen the stranger without knowing who he was or what he was doing.

First, in the ghostly lane, proving I have seen him once at least in my world, even if I don't remember it. There, he saved me from the full impact of the curse, drawing the larger part into himself. Then, the clearing that first week into the woods. And then? The wolves. No, wait! *After* the wolves. Only once we had safely disembarked from our makeshift boat did he appear, and then for but a moment.

I notice the pattern now. The pattern I had always been wary of, then talked myself around. Is the stranger helping? How many times have I asked myself this same question over the long journey? Is he helping? And I always answered myself: yes. I deluded myself into believing he was always there to help, because I longed for help so badly. But I can see the pattern now, and he never was. He was never there when we really needed him, only after. Where was he when the fire dryads scorched us? Where was he when the gem wolves ravaged or the mirrored hawks swooped low? Where was he when I was forced to let my friends stand alone against a horde of beasts? Was he there? No! He only came after. We had to survive all those perils on our own.

He said none of our hardships were my fault, and he is right. They do not lay at my door, but his. Reviewing all I have learned about this Creative One only cements the fact in my mind. All the tales Leal and Elden have told of his great power. He could have directed us which way to go from the start. He could have stopped any one of the attacks if he wanted to. Not only that, he could have prevented my beast of an uncle from cursing me in the first place. He was there. He could have ended this all before it began; he had the power. He chose not to use it. All the troubles of my life are on his hands.

The silence is not easy anymore. It is oppressive, and I must break it soon or break under it. "Why didn't you do anything? Why did you always stand aside and watch?" I have just challenged the greatest being in all the worlds, the mightiest of the Powers, and I know I should be frightened. But I do not feel fear. All I can feel is white-hot anger coursing through me.

"Giselle." The gentle way he calls my name wakes a yearning inside me. A yearning so strong my anger gives way. "My child, I have always been there. Did you never notice?"

Memories of loving care flood my mind. Papa

chasing me about the house, pretending he couldn't see where I went. Mother tucking me in at night with a song and a kiss. Ami baking sweets with me, making a royal mess of her mother's kitchen in the process. Healer Aliza doing up my hair and telling me how beautiful I looked. Bard Elric telling tales by the hearth when I managed to escape Uncle on long winter nights. And Eamon holding me, a smile on his lips and tenderness in his eyes.

Do you know me now, dear one?

I gasp, half starting up from my seat. Haldis, the helper who for so long wore a woman's voice, has now taken on a new one. She has transformed into the most loving voice in the world: his. So, it was him. He is the one who directed me this whole time—what to do, which way to go, how to help. He is the one who disclosed the use of my talisman. The one who saved my life, time and again.

He continues aloud, "Never did I leave when you had need of me. I have ever lent you my aid. I operated outside your vision for one simple reason: I was waiting to be asked. Yet you were so determined to do it on your own! You only broke down once. How else should my inklings know to rescue you from the fire? And even then, I was there, fighting a battle of my own. Think you the Dark Wizard was ever far from your camp? Nay. At every danger you faced, Rajani was there, and so was I."

The hollow gnawing of guilt and shame replaces the heat of my anger. I hang my head as I remember the two men struggling at the edge of a clearing while we bickered. I owe this man everything, my very life. And I have done nothing but take his food and berate him. I curl in on myself, wishing I could block his voice and my memory both. Wishing I could undo the past.

"As for the curse," he continues gravely, "do you truly think I care not? Was it not I who stood between you and the wrath of the Dark Power, letting only a small portion pass to you? For without this hardship, you would not have searched and found me in the searching. Even then, I did not leave you to face the trials alone. Did I not give you friends to walk alongside you, sharing in your troubles? Did I not stand with you every time you withstood the curse? And did I not give you even that weapon, which now hangs about your neck?"

I look down at my talisman. "My dreamsnare? It was passed to me through Ami from her mother."

"And to her from me. For she was an Enchantress, after all. You saw me that day in the market. Did you not?"

"Yes. Yes, My Lord, I did. Forgive me. I was wrong."

"It is already forgiven, dear one." His voice has gentled, and he sets a sun-weathered hand on my shoulder. "Yet, you must learn that things are not always as they appear. You are never alone, no matter how often it may seem that you are. For I will always be near you, though you do not see me. I always stand ready to lend aid. The aid may not come in a form you expect but come it will. All you must do is ask."

"Yes, My Lord. And I thank you. I thank you for all that you have done on my behalf."

He smiles. "That is well. And now, if you have finished refreshing yourself, the time has come to continue your quest. For you are near the end, indeed." He waves his arm to the west with a command. The trees spring apart on either side, creating a clear trail, carpeted in moss and roofed in leaves, leading straight on. "Follow this lane and you will find what you seek."

"Thank you once again, My Lord." I bow low and turn to the lane, but my feet stick fast to the springy moss. I find that I don't want to go. I don't want to walk away from this man who has loved me despite my weaknesses. Who has fought for me and guided me, even when I cast judgment against him. I would rather give my freedom, rather lose my family, to stay here in this land of magic with him.

"It is not walking away, dear one, it is walking toward. You shall live with me in time, but not now. I have much for you to do yet and many joys awaiting you ere you come to this glade again. I would not have you lose those who are anxiously awaiting your return. Go now."

I take a deep breath and nod. Squaring my shoulders, I force my right foot forward. Then my left, shuffling my way onward. I look behind only once and find that the trees have closed in where I passed. I force myself to a brisker pace. There is no going back.

19

FACING DEVORON

I stand in a dense fir grove well hidden amongst the wasted labyrinth of crags. Cold sweat dews my forehead as I stare into the dark, dank entrance of a cave, trying to muster up the last bit of courage it will take to go in. I know Devoron is down there, somewhere. The putrid stench from years of his decaying presence wafts up the passageway, burning my eyes. If that weren't enough to be sure of my goal, the gurgling hiss of his snore is unmistakable. Loud enough to beat heavily on my ears even from this distance.

Well, go in.

Haldis has returned to her usual nature, for which I am thankful. I would be far too intimidated to chat so casually with the Creative One himself.

Just one more minute.

Come now, Giselle. You've delayed nearly twenty already.

After making it all this way, will you accept your doom on the threshold ere it has fallen?

Her gentle words hold hard truth. I can't turn back now. Withdrawing my dreamsnare one final time for luck, I fumble it in shock. The talisman is completely clean! Every single strand a brilliant white.

"Thank you, Creative One." I breathe out an incredulous laugh, tucking my treasure safely back in my tunic.

I don't know when or how he did it, but his gift provides that last push I need to enter the menacing dark of the lair alone. Taking a deep breath, I drag my feet one small step over the threshold. Immediately, the dim green-tinted daylight of the forest vanishes, and I am swallowed in the void-black gullet of rock.

The clammy air presses in on me. I shudder but force my feet to shuffle along, adopting the odd gait to avoid a tragic misstep on the uneven ground. I think I am managing quite well, until my shin cracks against stone. I growl one of Uncle's favorite words under my breath and feel my way around the obstacle, only to bash into another at my side. Grumbling, I take one probing step after another until I reach the wall. I ought to be safe walking alongside it. But, alas, that is not to be. Whether by intent or natural design, the passages are choked with boulders. Though I strain my eyes to make them out, my trembling hand on the damp walls and Devoron's boneshaking snore serve much better guides as I grope my way through.

It is not long before I am chilled to the bone and bruised from heel to shin. And the further in I go, the worse the gag-inducing odor becomes. A steep decline takes me by surprise, and I tumble much further than I would have expected—as if this tunnel delves straight to the heart of the earth. The end comes abruptly. I land hard on my knees, the pain bringing tears to my eyes. But I clamp my teeth down on the scream fighting for release.

My only saving grace is that dim light now flickers through an opening to my left. It's a simple thing, but the marginal increase in visibility halves my fear. Shoving to my feet, I head for the glow. Let's get this over with.

I peek around the corner and there he is, looking just as I have always seen him in my nightmares. Eyes of fire, casting a grim light even through closed lids. A fearsome, predatory maw filled to the brim with razor-sharp teeth. A body of undulating words swirling about each other as they fade in and out, creating a smoky haze. A continuous morphing of his form, though most include a large set of wings and claws.

I edge into the room, aiming to hide myself from Devoron's keen senses as long as possible. But I'm focused so intently on him that I don't notice the jagged hole in the floor—until I plunge my foot in it and twist my ankle, that is. The jarring pain startles me so that I forget myself and cry out. Loudly. Complete with echoes.

Heart hammering like to break out of my chest, I clap a hand to my mouth and desperately hold my breath. At least now I don't have to smell him. The passing seconds drag like years as I cower in the gloom. But there is no answering hiss, no growl, nothing to suggest I have woken the monster. Gradually, I straighten, and finally allow myself to breathe easily again. I am safe...for the moment.

On the heels of this realization comes another: here is the monster I have set out to find, sound asleep right before me. I could kill him easily now and be free. If I do it quickly, he won't be able to put up a fight.

It may not be as satisfying an end as I had envisioned. Nor as noble. I cringe, thinking of the tongue-lashing Lord Elden would give me for even considering such a dishonorable tactic. But at least my odds of survival would be much improved over an attempt at combat. Crouching low, I hobble my way straight up to the beast and reach for the dagger at my side. Only to grope empty air.

Blast! How could I have forgotten? I left everything behind with Leal, nor did the Creative One offer me any weapon. An oversight...or a test? Either way, the result is me standing here at a loss. A muffled groan forces its way past my lips. All the effort to get down here, wasted. I debate staying anyway, though I would only be mauled in these close quarters when he wakes. I'll have a better advantage in the open. I must go back up.

Only, how am I to draw the monster out once I do?

While casting around for a solution, I notice a faint twinkling in the far corner and do a double take. Sure enough, an inkwell spider lies twitching on its side. How did the unfortunate thing find itself trapped all the way in here? I ease over and crouch to cradle the injured creature, gingerly pressing my finger to a gash in its side.

At my touch, it livens up and scurries down my arm to find a hiding spot in my trouser pocket. Poor thing. I'll see it's well taken care of. But first, I must finish this. Glancing at my ink-stained fingers, an idea springs to mind. Dipping my hands in the tiny black puddle, I write a message on the wall.

Leave now or die, your choice.

I have dreadful little hope he will leave, of course, but this should gain his attention, at least.

Now comes the laborious trudge through the boulder-strewn passages. I grit my teeth as pain slices through my hurt ankle with every step. The trip feels twice as long going back, but I refuse to rest, no matter how my leg aches. Delays now will do far more harm than good. Blinking fiercely, I claw my way out of the beastly hole at last. The pale, dappled sunlight blinds my sorely taxed eyes. Still, I've never been more grateful to see the sky. Fresh air wafts over me like a cleansing wave, and I draw in a deep breath, almost able to ignore the noisome smell clinging to my clothes.

I do allow myself a brief respite now, dropping to the

needle-blanketed earth just long enough to wrap my ankle. All the while, trying to come up with a better plan than waiting around to die. It will take a good deal more than swelling a river to flood point or cracking a cliff to rockslide for a battle of this magnitude. And this time, I am injured before the fighting begins. How can I possibly win? What can kill something so entrenched in the Dark Power?

I realize now my dagger would have been no use had it been present. My mind swirls frantically through every weapon I have ever heard of—not aided in the least by the fierce growls echoing from deep within the cave. Devoron has woken and apparently does not appreciate my heartfelt note.

Breath coming in short gasps, I double over as my heart beats a rapid tempo through my skull. I'm running out of time. And not one of the weapons I know will do any good against such an incorporeal creature. In desperation, I draw the dreamsnare from my tunic once again. It can give me whatever weapon I need. But which one can kill a monster of words and smoke? Which one? Which one!

Why not the one you hold now?

The world slows to a crawl as I register the obvious in Haldis' answer. What I need is exactly what I have always needed: the dreamsnare. Not to influence another object near me, but this time, the talisman itself. It *could* work. If Ami reconfigured it to pull Devoron from me in my own world, why could it not be made to act similarly here? But a snag immediately presents itself. The dreamsnare is so small. I couldn't entrap one of my inky friends with this, much less a beast of Devoron's bulk. Nor do I have the power to increase its reach. So how?

That's simple. Who has more power than you?

Of course! I've done it again, haven't I? I must remember that *I* don't have to do any of this. All I need to do is ask.

"Haldis, or er, Creative One. Um, whichever you are now. Please, will you l-lend me just...just one small portion of your strength?" I stumble over my words as I let my guard down fully for the first time in my life.

A jolt of molten power surges through me from somewhere deep inside, tingling along my arms and out my hands. The sensation is odd, but not unpleasant. And slowly, the net begins to grow. My victorious shout rings through the wood...and is met with a vicious snarl from just within the tunnel.

My heart leaps to my throat.

Oh, faster. Please go faster!

Another surge of power shoots through me and the talisman balloons to several times the size of a common fishing net. I sigh in relief. It should be enough. At my unspoken command, the net lifts high in the air, hovering above the cave entrance and casting a barrier across the stars. One strand snakes around an overhanging branch and latches onto a thin limb at shoulder height, creating a rough lever for release. I need only untie the rope, or in a scrape, break the limb.

The trap is set just in time.

Devoron charges from his lair with a roar. For a moment, only his blazing eyes are visible in the dark of the cave's mouth—made even darker by the gathering gloom of night. But as he advances, I can clearly make out the terrible guises he adopts. His shifting form morphs dizzyingly from a griffin, to a winged lion, then a great winged fox. Finally, it settles on an enormous wyvern. His new wings stretch up almost as high as my trap among the treetops.

"Well now, the foolisssh wench has finally arrived. I must admit, I am impressed you have sssurvived long enough to come this far. Yet, you did not truly think your note could frighten me, did you, girl?"

I have not heard his voice for such a very long time. It ravages me anew, bringing back all my most torturous memories. I flinch and he laughs. It is disorienting to hear this mocking in my ears rather than echoing within my head. A simple fact. Ironically, the disorientation grounds me and strips away a large portion of Devoron's power. He is no longer the all-consuming terror he once was. Nonetheless, a terror he is still.

"Not at all," I reply, doing my best to sound confident. It takes a good deal of effort. Confidence is a far cry from my accustomed state. "I didn't expect you to have quite that much sense. But even you deserve a chance." No need to tell him I nearly didn't give it.

"Is that so?" His blazing eyes light with vicious mirth, unnerving me.

Stand firm, dear one.

The soft whisper steadies me, centers me. I raise my head to meet the monster's mockery.

"A chance?" His gleeful cackling grates on my ears. "Why should I need a chance? What can *you* possibly do to *me*? You are a worthlesss, pathetic disgrace."

"I'm not." I shrink even as I defy him, but I do not back down.

"You are! You are worthlesss. Friendlesss. Even weaponlesss. You cannot defeat me. What power do you have, puny maiden? No one is coming to save you. No one ever has. You are always alone."

"Lies! I am not alone. I never have been." It is not so hard to sound fierce now. Anger can do that, I'm told. "Nor am I worthless. I thought so once. You will never convince me so again. Who says *I* need awesome power to defeat you? I have the strongest of all Powers on my side. He has already driven your master away. Do you want him to cast you out as well?"

"So, my massster has been driven out? That may be. Yet, it does not follow that he has been finissshed. Do not think he is gone for good. He always returns to me after a time." Though Devoron gloats, he does not sound as sure of himself as before.

"If he does, you will not be here to see it," I sneer. "As I said before, you may leave now or die, the choice is yours."

"And what is this pitifully desperate plan of yours?"

"Look up. Do you know what that is?"

"A mass of cord." His tone is dismissive, but his body begins to swirl chaotically, betraying his agitation.

"It is a dreamsnare. Have you never heard of them? Your one bane?" I inch toward the lever, hoping my monologue will be enough distraction to spring the trap. "Dreamsnare strips away every thought you have ever consumed. You will be left hollow, bare, just a speck of fire in the nothingness. Your own life force will easily snuff you out. So, you have two options. You can be cast out with your master—and face the prospect of starvation in the void without a host—or you can choose the dreamsnare, a swift and yet more permanent death."

I have no idea if it's true, of course. The term 'draw the monster out' is rather broad. But it sounds convincing. And right now, that's all that matters. I lay a hand gently on the lever, ready in case my bluff goes awry.

Devoron spins from side to side, his gruesome head cocked at an unnatural angle. Several agonizing moments pass before he stills. "Rajani, Most Illustrious Wizard of the Dark Power himself, has placed me here. There is no Power in existence who can go against hisss will!" He blasts toward me with the full force of a winter storm. A power I never knew he possessed.

Swept off my feet, my hand torn from the lever, I'm thrown two feet away, thrust against the bowl of a tree with a sickening crack. I'm fairly sure I just broke my freshly healed ribs, and my ankle is not thanking me. I scream in futile frustration. I'll never make my way back to the trap in this gale. There is nothing I can cast that will hit its mark. But then a dark streak tears across my vision. I hadn't noticed the spider leave my pocket. But there it is, clinging to the lever by a tightly wound inky thread. I can't see clearly what is happening, but all at once, the giant net crashes to the ground, suffocating my lifelong tormentor.

The lashing wind dies abruptly. Devoron's chaotic mass writhes within the net's confines, fiery wisps flickering at the edges, and my heart drops to my toes. It's not going to work. He will escape, and it will all be for naught. But just as I grow sure of my hopeless plight, he emits an ear-piercing, bone-chilling screech...and vanishes.

Panting, hardly able to believe my eyes, I stumble over to the trap. Amidst the ink-black words of ideas and the colorful swirls of memory still lies the smallest flaming spark of life. I hear movement behind me and step aside as He comes to finish the job.

"Begone, foul creature of the dark abyss, and trouble my daughter no more."

At his word, Devoron burns out and is gone.

He turns to me. "You have done exceedingly well,

dear one. Take now what you wish, and I shall dispose of the rest."

"Thank you. I have something for you, too." Turning to the shambles of the trap, I coax the injured spider into my palm and hold it out.

He takes it carefully in his creased hands. "Ah, you have found Stella."

"They have names?"

"Everything has a name, child. From the brightest star to the smallest ant. It was she who found you first at the edge of the wood. Keeping hold of her has proven troublesome ever since. She's taken quite a liking to you." He smiles down at the creature cuddling into his cupped hand. "Rest easy now, my small one. Your friend is going home."

I carefully collect my belongings from the netting and sift through them. The poor ideas I replace and the good ones I scatter to the winds, where they will fly until I need them again.

"Now, child," he says, placing a hand on each of my shoulders, "are you prepared to return and face what is awaiting you?"

"Yes, I am more than ready to get home. Thank you, once again, for everything." I close my eyes and feel him place his gentle hands on my head in a blessing, and I am falling. I'm falling through feathers. This time, I fall for what feels like ages. Home must be much farther than I thought.

But at last I feel the coarse homespun pillow behind my head and a warmth surrounding me which I haven't felt in the longest time. I open my eyes to see Ami's face hovering over mine with a smile so big it nearly splits her in two.

"Praise be to the Power! That dreamsnare tore nearly an hour ago and you still wouldn't wake."

Eamon is pressing close behind her. "Welcome home, Giselle."

20

HOMECOMING

"Look who's back!" Gil enters the room and pulls a chair up near my bed, tipping backwards with his feet propped by mine. "I want to hear the whole tale." He spans his arms out, indicating how long he expects this tale to be, and nearly topples himself over. Just as he regains his balance, the twins come barreling through and knock him to the ground. Calling apologies as Ami reprimands them, they shove through the door.

I laugh as I reach down to help him up. "The story will have to wait for a moment. I'm sorry to ask it, Ami, but do you have any food at hand? I'm famished."

"And you ought to be after fasting nearly five days." She shakes a finger at me as she rises from her stool. "I'll have you know, I've been to a good deal of trouble saving you from dehydration." Eamon takes her place by my side.

"Has it only been five days?" I ask. "I count a month at the least."

"A month! How did you survive without food for a month?" Gil looks aghast. He thinks he's on the brink of starvation if he misses one meal.

"I had food, Gil." I laugh. "But I suppose it was all in my head."

"I am sure the food of that world was sufficient for a body in that world," Eamon muses. "It may not have all been in your head, in that sense." He's putting more thought into this than I expected. Perhaps he has been more worried than he lets on.

"It still wasn't proper food, though, was it?" Ami returns with one hand on her hip and the other holding a bowl. "Not like my good, thick porridge." She has always been quite proud of her porridge, insisting it is far better than her mother's. And though I'll never admit it, she's right.

"Thank you." I reach out eagerly, but my smile sags when I look at the contents. It's quite a meager portion.

"I know it doesn't look like much, but you'll be surprised at how little will satisfy after a fast that long. You may not even finish this much." She jabs her ladle in my direction. "So, don't overdo it."

"Yes, ma'am."

"Tell us about the battle," Gil insists when I have swallowed but a spoonful.

"Gilpin!" Ami hits him over the head with her ladle. "Let the poor thing eat in peace."

"You could pass the time by giving me a tale," I suggest. "What has happened since I've been away? Was Uncle horrid?"

"Well, he wasn't as bad as he could have been," Gil hedges.

"I'd say he's been a fair menace," Eamon grunts.

"True," Gil admits, "but that first night was rather amusing. Honestly, he didn't even consider I might have ulterior motives when I began buying him drinks. The entire tavern was abuzz with the novelty, and he didn't give it a thought. Already too far gone to notice!"

"I wager it was not so amusing when you had to carry him home. Was it, brother dear?"

Gil just shrugs.

"I wouldn't say that," Eamon answers for him. "I found it quite good fun. That is, until you thought it my duty to assist him."

"Well, you didn't expect me to do it, did you?" Ami raises her ladle again.

Eamon covers his head, backtracking quickly. "Oh, no. Certainly not! I would never ask you to do something so troublesome."

"I still say we ought to have just dropped him in the field." Gil shakes his head. "Or better yet, the pigsty!"

"He has earned it several times over," Eamon agrees, and both men laugh uproariously.

Ami rolls her eyes and speaks over them. "To answer your question properly, Giselle, he did come 'round once he was sober enough to notice you were gone. Not that he stayed sober long. He didn't do much real damage, not with my father on his way home and the boys here to keep him in check. Though, he did frighten the twins half to death."

"Which is a surprisingly hard thing to do," Gil quips.

I laugh, nearly choking on my last bite of porridge and wave Eamon off before he starts pounding my back. I have hardly recovered and set down my bowl when Gil pounces.

"So, the tale?"

"Yes, yes." I throw up my hands in mock exasperation. "Peace! I'll tell you." I fight a sly grin. Let's see how long I can lead him on. Most of my time was spent trudging through an endless expanse of trees, after all. Hardly the most interesting subject matter. I take a deep breath and begin.

"Well, let's see. First, I woke in the mind world and traveled through a wasteland to the nearest town. There, I made some friends who escorted me on a truly miserable trek through the local wood. I very much would not recommend a holiday there. And then I left them to explore the mountain range myself. Turns out, highland passes are quite bleak and treacherous. Though it was all made worthwhile when I met the Creative One at the top—"

"The Creative One?" Eamon perks up, eyes shining. "You met the Creative One? As in, face to face?"

I nod. "We shared a meal and then he sent me home." I end with a shrug, nearly cracking at the dumbfounded look on Gil's face.

"And that's it? That is all that happened for a month? What about the fighting!"

I can't keep the mirth tamped down any longer and feel my smile might break my face in two. "Oh! Oh, you meant about the fighting." I nudge his foot with mine. "Well, I did my fair share of that as well. Rajani was quite determined to keep me from my goal and had plenty of minions at his disposal. And then there was Devoron himself, though the Creative One did most of the work there. But I did drown a few wolves all on my own." The smug tone in my voice is unmistakable.

Gil whoops and Eamon claps me on the shoulder. "That's my girl," he whispers in my ear.

I grin up at him and then turn back to Gil, unable to pass up the opportunity for one final jab. "I must say, you were worse than any of the monsters. Incessant chattering, knocking most of our packs into the river, picking fruit you shouldn't. You were quite the nuisance."

"So, nothing new there then." Ami laughs.

"No, not much has changed." I wink.

Gil crosses his arms, huffing good-naturedly. "You're just sore that I'm a better fighter than you."

I laugh. "Perhaps. Much as it pains me to admit, you did save my life at least once. But that chapter will have to wait for later."

"Aww, no." Gil throws dignity to the wind and drops to his knees, hands clasped in front of him. "Finish the tale properly. Please?"

"Get up, man!" Eamon pulls him to his feet. "She has more important things to do today."

"Yes," I sigh, "It's time I settled matters with Uncle."

That sobers even Gil. All trace of merriment dies in the heavy air as I slowly get to my feet. I wasn't expecting the weakness in my knees and nearly drop back to the bed. But Eamon catches me, and after a few rounds of the room with his support, I'm steady enough to move on my own—though he still shadows my every step.

Gil claps me on the shoulder, and Ami silently squeezes my hand as I pass. I nearly run into their father just outside the door. His face lights up as he catches me by the arm. "Why, good morning, Giselle! It's good to see you up again."

"Yes, Bard Elric. It's good to be up."

"Would you like assistance home?"

"No, thank you." I gesture at Eamon. "I can manage."

His eyes crinkle, and he pats my arm gently. "Very well, then. But should you need anything, you just send word, and my boys will come running." He pauses, then adds more softly, "I'll not be losing another member of this family."

I can't find the words to answer him, so I simply nod thanks with tears in my eyes and move on. My feet drag as if they are not yet ready to face what I know I must. Biting my lip, I trudge on. Eamon swiftly moves to my side, slipping his arm through mine to lend his strength but keeping his silence. As we approach the door, I force myself to straighten.

Stopping outside, I gulp and whisper to Eamon. "Wait here, please."

His grip tightens on my arm. "I am not letting you go in there alone."

The tenderness in his tone nearly sets my tears loose. I turn to him, placing a hand against his chest to hold him back. "I know you want to protect me, and I love you for it. But this is something I have to do myself."

"Giselle."

"Please, Eamon. I promise you I won't be alone."

He grunts in confusion, but nods assent. "If you must." Glaring in Uncle's general direction, he adds, "I will be waiting right here, all the same. Call if you need anything." Releasing his grip on my arm, he brushes a hand softly over my cheek before stepping back several paces. He stands as if taking root, still as carven stone with arms crossed and his intense grey eyes nearly boring holes through the door.

I smile gratefully at his determination, turn to the door, take a deep breath, and enter.

21

A FINAL CONFRONTATION

I t is dark inside. The shutters bolted. A sure sign Uncle is home and in poor state. He prefers living in a dismal hole when coming off a binge—as if his sharpening mind demands penance for his wrongs. The fire has obviously gone unlit for quite some time. Cold ashes are strewn about, coating everything in grime. The remains of several days' breakfast clutter the table, and the air reeks of spirits. But the room is otherwise empty.

"Uncle," I call hesitantly.

Moving toward his room, I trip over a bottle and nearly fall flat on my face. It skids across the floor, bashing against the larder door and eliciting a low grunt from within. I find myself intensely grateful I won't be staying for a meal. Another grunt, drawn out this time, followed by the sound of shifting feet. Then the door is jerked nearly off its hinges, and Uncle's bulk looms in the opening.

"Whozit? Whara you wan," he slurs as he stumbles into the room. Even I have never seen him this bad before. He must have been at the bottle every minute since I left.

He crashes into the table, effectively stopping his progress amongst the filth, and fumbles for a match. In the small radius of light cast, I see him clearly. I'm expecting simply an unkempt, very hungover, drunk. What I see is a specter. Sagging skin, wan as the candle he holds in his shaking hand. Matted hair evoking more the image of a wild beast than a man. Veined bloodshot eyes squint down into my face. In the span of a week, he has grown truly revolting. Small wonder the twins were frightened.

However, he seems just as taken aback at the sight of me. Shocked sober enough to resume his abrasive manner, if not with all his usual vigor, he snarls. "Well, look who decided to come crawling back. Your worthless friends finally turn you out, did they?"

"No. I chose to come."

"I suggest you choose to get a move on with the cleaning up then, you lazy wench. Just look at the state of my home," he growls, gesturing wildly about him.

"Yes," I reply stiffly. "I can see you have not coped well in my absence. A fate you are doomed to grow accustomed to, I'm afraid."

"How's that then?"

I take a deep breath, steeling my spine. "I'm leaving, Uncle." I step around him to my room. "And I will not be returning."

He laughs. "You ain't leaving."

"And why not?" I demand, hot ire rising within me. "You have said often enough I am not worth your trouble. Now we shall both be unburdened."

"You haven't got the gall to walk away. Not when you're needed here. I know you, girl, you'd never leave kin behind."

True, I would never abandon kin. Yet he errs to remind me. For we are not kin. Not anymore. Not since the day I learned he cursed me. I've chosen new kin, and it's there I'm needed.

I stomp on and he follows, watching with shifty eyes as I gather my few belongings. His face clouds in confusion then settles into a mask of rage when he finally registers that I am in earnest. As I push back past him, he grabs my arm, twisting so hard it's like to snap.

"I said, you ain't leaving. I forbid it."

I long to strike him. But no matter how much I have learned of fighting in the past month and a fortnight, or five days, or however long it has been since I last saw his hideous face, I know I will never win against Uncle in a fistfight. So, I settle for threats. "Remove your hand...or you might just lose it."

He draws back from the ice in my voice, or perhaps

it's the fire in my glare. I have never been this sure before. My sudden confidence robs him of his. For the first time in my life, the man with the acidic voice is at a complete loss for words.

I waste no time pressing the advantage. "You don't understand, do you? I broke your curse! I killed that monster you forced upon me, and with it, my bonds to you. You cannot cage me here any longer. I'm leaving."

My assertion recalls the acidic voice to full force. "The abyss you are," he roars, lumbering after me with upraised fists. Thank the Power, his drunken aim is off! The blow that would have laid me out slams me against the wall instead. My head hits hard. The metallic tang of blood fills my mouth. But I keep my feet.

Another blow, cracking wood this time as the outer door bursts open, startling us both. Eamon's strapping form is ringed in sunlight. He strides purposefully over and shoves his way in front of me. A bulwark against this maelstrom.

"Lay hands on her again and it's me you'll answer to, filth."

Bloodshot eyes glare at him with deep hatred, then turn on me. "You selfish little harlot."

It takes my knight only one strike to lay the monster low, writhing in the mucky filth of his hovel. Shaking with rage, Eamon holds out a hand. I grasp it firmly, trying to convey I'm all right. Keeping his eyes trained on the threat, he ushers me in front of him. "Come, love, we're going home." His voice is raw, and his hands still shake as he leads me to the mangled door.

I go gladly yet am compelled to stop at the threshold.

Hold, child. I hear the Creative One's voice clear as any spoken word. *Do not leave it like this.*

I sigh. "What would you have me do?"

Eamon's furrowed brow reminds me not to carry on these conversations aloud. He must think I hit my head quite hard indeed. I give him a reassuring smile but put out a hand to forestall his questions. Closing my eyes, I listen.

I would have you forgive. One day, this man will need your help, and I would have you give it.

Flabbergasted, my eyes pop open to stare at Uncle. He has crawled back to his knees, red-tinged spittle dribbling from the corner of his mouth. And I find that in this moment, I truly loathe him. I despise this man who cursed me, who told me I was worthless, who beat me without cause. He has so much penance to pay. Forgive him? Help him? I think not.

In my bitterness, I am bold enough to make excuses to the greatest of all Powers. This time speaking within my mind.

Why would you ask this of me? He has not even asked it for himself. He is not sorry for any of the wrong he has done. Why should he be absolved? The monster does not deserve it!

His reply is full of tender understanding. *Oh, my dearest, forgiveness is not for the transgressor only, but the one who was wronged as well. It may ease his guilt but will set you free.*

That makes no sense.

So much has changed since I was last in this room. Devoron is gone. There is no longer a hissing voice in my head. No longer fire behind my eyes nor daggers through my skull. My thoughts no longer vanish as I think them.

I am already free!

Most importantly, there is a new voice in my mind. A loving one that never truly left, and I know never will. One that taught me the power of creating alongside him.

You yourself made me so.

Trust me, my child, there is more to bondage than curses only. It is true, I set you free, yet you must also decide to free yourself. Free yourself from the chains of hatred. Show mercy. For even the worst man may mend, if given a chance. But should he not, that is no concern of yours. Your only concern is the way in which you act. A monster you have called him. Do not, then, transform yourself to match such a monster. Doing so will only bring death. Here you choose your destiny. Choose life, my child. Life unfettered and free.

I would scoff if the evidence of his words were not so clearly before my eyes. How had this pathetic drunkard become the terror of my life? He held on to anger. He refused to forgive, and bitterness brought him a living death in consequence—one he passed to me. Is that the new life I want? To spread a cycle of hate through my children, and them theirs? Perhaps, I truly must forgive a monster to avoid becoming one. And though it seems a simple answer, the practice is harder than I would have thought.

Locking my gaze with his, I speak aloud. "Uncle," I grit my teeth, not sure I can do this after all. Eamon makes a strangled sound deep in his throat and tugs gently at my hand. I reach out to calm him once more, then force the words out. "I am leaving, with no intent to return...but...I...I forgive you."

"I don't ask your forgiveness, traitor, nor do I need it."

I manage a wavering smile. "No, but another asks it for you." I finally take that last step into the light, calling back over my shoulder, "Farewell, Uncle," and close the door.

❧ 22 ❧

THE LIGHT

Eamon draws me to him as I crumple in the outermost garden and weep. He holds me tightly, paying no mind to the blood and tears now staining his clothes. Oh, by the Power, I don't deserve this man. I cling to him all the same, his strong arms the only thing holding me together as I crumble to a million tiny pieces. Brushing my tangled hair from my face, he whispers soothing words in my ear, assuring me that all will be well. My wailing only grows worse. He eventually falls silent, though his warm hands never cease their calming caresses.

I don't know how long we sit there in the muck, but a good deal later, Eamon stands. "Come, love. Let's get you away from here."

I nod, staring up at him through a watery veil, yet I can't find the strength to follow. So, lifting me in his arms, he makes for the edge of the village. I don't know where he's taking me. I don't much care. The easy rhythm of his steps slowly calms me. My sobs abate to whimpers, then sniffles, and finally reduce to an exhausted silence. He walks steadily on. I let my eyes drift closed. Turning my head into his shoulder, I doze off.

I wake to a steady murmur. That of water rushing over stones. I needn't look to know where we are. Our spot by the river. The place where this all began. I feel Eamon's calm presence behind me. It takes several tries to draw my swollen eyes open. When I manage it, I notice I'm lying on top of the man, my fisted hand still clutching his tunic. I groan and force my stiff fingers to open.

Eamon chuckles, supporting me as I ease into a more dignified position. "Feel better?"

"Yes...and no. Why does it ache so when I have just gained all I wanted? What is wrong with me?"

"Don't, Giselle." He gently pulls my hands from my face, ducking to catch my eye as I shift away. "Listen to me, you did nothing wrong. Whatever else he is, that man raised you. He is the only blood kin you have left. You've a right to mourn this ending."

"Truly?"

"Truly, love. No one would fault you."

His words are a balm to my shattered soul. I lay my head on his snot-encrusted shoulder, fingering the soiled garment. It's his favorite—the one he is so careful to keep away from the forge—and now I've ruined it.

"You might fault me yet. Just look at the state of your tunic."

"Don't fret over it." He lowers my hand but keeps it clasped in his. "I may be a poor blacksmith, but I'm not yet so destitute I can't afford a new tunic."

I laugh and the tightness in my chest begins to ease. "Perhaps I'll make you a new one, free of charge." It's as good as a marriage proposal, and we both know it.

"Well, I won't say no to that."

Sighing, I sink into his arms and we watch the river. It's the first time in a long while I don't have a pressing concern, no place to go, and I'm content to just be still together. But Eamon has something on his mind.

"Say, love," he asks after a few minutes, "what were you doing when you stopped at the door?"

"What do you mean?"

"Before you told Ackley you forgave him? The look on your face...well, it's driving me mad."

"Oh, that. I was...arguing...with the Creative One." My smile wavers slightly. "He asked me to forgive Uncle, and at first, I didn't want to."

His eyes grow wide as silver coins. "But you do now? You can truly forgive him for all of it? No reservations. Just forget the last thirteen years of your life ever happened?"

"Maybe not forget. But I am trying to forgive," I

hesitate, "trying hard. Which ought to be the same thing, but I know it's not." I sigh, turning to him, needing him to understand. "This is not something I feel I want to do, but something I know I must. And not only because the Creative One asked it of me. I *need* to be better than Uncle was, Eamon. If I don't do this...I'm frightened I will become just like him: filled with spite, bitterness, despair. I can't let that happen."

"Oh, Giselle, I am so proud of you," he whispers. "I do not think I could be that strong. Truly, his wrongs were not against me, and yet, I'm not likely to ever forgive them."

"Perhaps one day you will. If the Creative One asks it of you, I'm sure you will."

"Then will you tell me more? About you and the Creative One?"

"Ah, for that, I think I'll need to start at the beginning."

He shrugs. "I've nowhere else to be."

So, I start, telling the tale properly this time. As I go on, my voice grows stronger. The pain of today fading as I recall all that happened to me in another world. Yet, as my tale unfolds, Eamon gradually withdraws. It starts small, a wavering in his gaze, a slight shifting away from me. At first, I attribute it to the restlessness that comes from sitting still on the hard stone too long. But when he drops my hand, just as I'm telling of that last mad escape with Leal, I know something is gravely wrong.

The light returns to his eyes when I recount meeting with the Creative One, but they do not quite meet mine. And when the tale is finished, the smile he bestows on me is forced. A smile of the lips only, but not the eyes. Something in him has shut down, and I don't know why.

"That's good, Giselle. You did well." He does get up now, stretching as he walks to a nearby tree.

"Eamon?" I stand too, trying hard to catch his eye.

He clears his throat and turns away. "Well, you are free now. Of this monster and your uncle. Where do you plan to go? I don't think staying at Gil's permanently is the best idea."

"Now that," I walk to him, laying a hand on his arm, "depends very much on where you plan to be."

His jaw clenches, eyes trained firmly on the tree in front of him. "Are you sure you still want me?"

I draw a sharp breath. "Of course, I still want you. How could you think otherwise?"

"Well, I'm certainly no lord, am I?" His voice has taken on a harsh edge and I recoil.

"Why should that matter?"

Is he...jealous? No, not Eamon. He would never be so petty. There must be something else.

"Eamon, please, tell me what's wrong."

He is quiet for a moment, then shakes his head, tone gentling. "I'm nothing but a simple blacksmith. I haven't got much to my name." He finally meets my eyes. The pain and longing I read in them clutch at my heart. But they are quickly replaced with the steel of resolve. "You shouldn't still want me, Giselle. You don't need me anymore. And now that you've seen far better offers..." He trails off, then continues in a whisper, voice nearly cracking on the last word. "You deserve far better than me."

Ah, there it is. Not jealousy but fear. Fear and doubt. Stifling inadequacy. Feelings with which I am all too familiar—though not ones I thought Eamon would know. Yet he's bolstered me so many times. Perhaps I can do the same for him now.

"Oh, Eamon, no. That is not true. Lord Elden was your counterpart. If I've seen anything, it's that I'll never find a better man. You've always been there for me. Even when you could not stay by my side physically, you came in spirit. No amount of coin can outweigh that. I don't know what I'd do without you."

I reach for him again, and he pulls away, tearing his eyes from mine. Distancing himself, though I can see how it pains him to do so. If there is one thing I know about this man, it is that he will always do what's best for me, no matter the cost to himself. Yet I never thought to see the day when I had to convince Eamon what is best for me is him.

I square my shoulders. "Eamon, hear me now." My voice rings with a resolve to match his. "I could live in a castle with a banquet every night and servants to give me all that I wished and still be no happier than I was with my uncle. Because things are worth nothing without love.

"Nobility is not about what you *have*, it is who you *are*. It is what you do. The way you treat those around you. It is what you give. How you give of yourself when there's nothing else left.

"I learned many things on my quest. One of the most devastating lessons was how deceptive appearances tend to be. The most ornate and enticing things at face value were also the most perilous. All of which paled in comparison to the simplicity of the beauty in the glade behind the falls.

"To the rest of the world, you may appear only a poor blacksmith, but I have always known you to be a far better man than many twice your rank." I cup his face in my hands, forcing him to meet my gaze once more. "Smith or lord, it makes no difference to me. It's Eamon, the man I want. Eamon, the man I *need*. And nothing is ever going to change that."

A tense silence stretches between us as emotions war across his face. My eyes never waver from his, attempting to pour all the love and hope I have into him. I know the moment he breaks through the prison of doubt. His eyes fill with tenderness, and his mouth breaks into that crooked half-smile I love so well as he wraps me in an embrace.

"Thank you." He sighs into my hair. "I suppose you were not the only one who needed to be reminded of their worth. I'm sorry if I hurt you. You do know that I will always want you?"

"Yes, I know." I melt against him, shocked at my own daring. Relieved it worked. And desperately hoping I never have to do it again.

"And I truly am so immensely proud of you, my love. I couldn't imagine going through half the things you've done. Nor coming out of it with such strength. Would that I could speak with the Creative One as you do."

He has hardly finished his wish when another voice speaks from nearby. "And so you shall."

"Creative One!" I spring away from Eamon, who drops to his knees with head bowed.

"Arise." He speaks genially, not so much an order as a request. When Eamon has regained his composure, the Creative One turns and addresses me. "You have done well, my child, and you are learning swiftly, though I do not pretend your road will be easy. You will struggle greatly at times. But when you do, remember, I will always be there to aid you. Though you do not see me, I will be there."

"Yes, My Lord. I will remember."

"I have a gift to help you do so." From his pocket, the Creative One pulls an inkwell spider.

As I cradle it in my hands, I notice a small scratch stretching all the way down one side. "Is this...?"

"Yes, Stella has been inconsolable since you left. She followed you throughout the wood and cannot resign herself to saying farewell now. She won't leave you and won't forget. Use her well, for the more you do, the greater she will grow."

"I—I thank you, My Lord," I breathe, barely forming the words in my shock. I step back, cradling my precious charge. "Really, Stella, making this kind of a journey when you're still hurt. What's gotten into you?"

"And you, my son." The Creative One turns back to Eamon. "You who have followed me for so long. You are to be commended on your steadfast opposition of this man's wrongdoing in favor of one for whom you care. Yet one day the man may come, seeking reconciliation. Do not, then, fail your friends in this trial. For judging too quickly and showing no mercy to one who has it in his heart to become a better man may bring only destruction."

"Yes, My Lord," Eamon responds gravely. "Though I do not trust the man, if she wishes at that time to see him again, I will still stand by her."

"It is well. You shall learn in time." He spreads his arms out over us, palms facedown above our heads. "And now, my dear ones, go in peace."

I glance up, and he is gone. With Eamon's arm around me and Stella nestled safely in my hands, I smile. I am free. And I am loved. Now, it is time to start living the life I have imagined.

❦ 23 ❦

THE TUNIC AND THE ARMBAND

The life I imagined did not involve being woken at the break of dawn by two chattering boys. On this particular morning, however, I don't mind. I am more excited than the twins for once, if less inclined to talk. Rubbing sleep from my eyes, I let them drag me into the bright kitchen. The sweet scent of baking rides the gentle breeze blowing in at the window.

Both boys release me to dive for the plate of still-steaming tarts sitting on the table. Gil is already there with a tart in each hand. The three of them drip jam and crumbs, all the while proclaiming the perfection of Ami's work. She has been trying for days to replicate her mother's special recipe. Looks like she finally succeeded.

She beams as she turns to me. "I promised they would be ready the day of your wedding."

"And you have kept your word." I take one of the coveted sweets. Biting into it gently, my intended decorum evaporates as the sticky filling oozes over my chin. I try to wipe it off but only manage to smear the mess more.

"Oh yes, you look the part of a bride now," Gil jests, wiping his face off with one of Ami's towels.

She thumps him over the head with her rolling pin, none too gently. "She'll look a queen by the time I'm through with her."

I'm not entirely sure if that's a compliment to me or simply an indication of her skill. So rather than reply, I stick my tongue out at Gil. "And I'm afraid no amount of help will ever make you look a proper groom's aid."

"Speaking of," Ami says, raising her rolling pin again, "aren't you overdue to meet Eamon?"

Gil jumps from his chair. "Quite right! I'd better be off." He grabs hold of the twins. "Come along, boys. We best leave the womenfolk to get ready if we know what's good for us. You can help put up the arbor with Father." They groan as they're dragged out the door.

Not long after they leave, there's a knock and Eamon's mother comes in. "Good morning, my dearies!" She hugs me tight. "Are you ready for the big day, love?"

"A bit nervous, actually, Mother Finola." I am ever so thankful to her for stepping in a week after the troth pledging. These past few months have been stressful enough. I'm not sure Ami and I would have survived each other if left to ourselves. And it has been nice to have a mother again. For both of us.

"Well, then. Let's see if we can get you relaxed with a bath."

"We'll need rosewater," Ami demands. "All brides bathe in rosewater the day of their wedding."

Mother Finola winks at me before turning to Ami. "Then it's a good thing I run the best florist shop in the county."

For the next several hours, I'm scrubbed and scraped, poked and prodded, pulled and pushed, as my two bride's aids do their best to make me presentable. I don't pay much attention to what they are doing. I've never been one for the finer arts of beauty. But listening to them debate the virtues of braids over curls brings a smile I can't shake. What they end up giving me is a twist of braids that appears both elegant and simple, with ribbons of deep sage woven in to match my dress. At long last, I'm pronounced ready.

The traditional embroidered gown draws a crowd as we head out of the village, forming a procession of well-wishers. Harmless enough, yet I fight an undercurrent of worry. I have not seen Uncle since a day after I left him, at which point it was made abundantly clear what would happen to him should he come for me again. And though he has kept his distance, a gathering this loud is sure to garner his attention, no matter how inebriated he is. I don't breathe easy until we reach the tree line.

It's not often done, but Eamon and I agreed to hold a private ceremony. Just his family and mine—Ami's family, that is—at our special place by the river. It is quite a romantic gesture, but I ought to have considered the difficulty of arriving there without soiling my clothes, especially with the sharp descent into the clearing. The day is quite warm for a brisk autumn, and I'm likely to have more than a happy glow by the time I wed. I only hope all the work spent on my hair isn't undone before Eamon gets to see it.

But none of that matters when I see him, and I catch my breath. I don't believe he has ever looked better than he does right now in the tunic I made him, a pale blue on which Ami insisted, with his hair slightly a mess and waiting for me under an arbor filled with the last of summer's blooms. He smiles as I meet him, and my heart is like to burst.

"Giselle, you look—" He pauses.

"Stunning," Gil offers from beside the river.

"You look—" Eamon still can't seem to find the right word, but his eyes say it all.

"Or you could try enchanting," Gil continues, "ravishing, angelic. Come on, man, pick one!"

I laugh. "Thank you. You don't look so bad yourself."

"Well, thanks for that," Gil replies. "You could at least call me dashing."

I roll my eyes and Eamon snorts. Pulling me close, he whispers, "You look lovely."

"And you, my love," I whisper back, fingering the embroidery at his neckline, "look dashing."

He chuckles. "You did a fine job."

"I did, didn't I?"

And now there is no more time for chat as our family gathers around. Ami marches the twins back to their place, soaked from playing in the river. Eamon's sister stands between their parents, recently married herself and heavy with child. Bard Elric steps up behind us into the arbor, ready to perform the ceremony. And Gil comes to stand at Eamon's side. All my family is here.

But I catch movement from the corner of my eye and stiffen. Yes, indeed, all my family is here. Uncle stands deep amid the trees, unnoticed by all but me.

Do not fear, my child. I have brought him, and he will cause no trouble.

Still uneasy, I glance back. Yet, truly, Uncle is looking far better than he did the last time I saw him. He may, in fact, be sober for once. When he sees I've noticed him, he puts his hands up, palms out in a placating gesture, and takes a step back. Perhaps he truly has begun to change in the months of my absence.

I sigh and try to relax as Bard Elric begins reciting a litany to the Creative One, followed by the Rites. Most of which I don't fully hear. But as I lock eyes with Eamon, all my worry flees, and I can't concentrate on anything but him. I come back to myself at the Binding, when he withdraws an armband from his pocket. It's a simple thing of burnished copper, though masterfully crafted with elegant curls at each end. Blushing slightly, he gently slips it in place just below my right shoulder, marking me as his for the rest of our lives.

As the Blessing of the Bard concludes the ceremony, Uncle catches my eye again. He bows, raises his hand in farewell, and then disappears into the trees.

I smile as I brush a hand over my armband. I have a new family, now and forever.

Leaning into Eamon, I whisper, "You did a fine job."

He smirks. "I did, didn't I?"

As the last notes of the Blessing drift away on the wind, Eamon pulls me close and kisses me amidst the shouts of our family. I have never felt more loved or more worthy.

EPILOGUE: TEN YEARS LATER

"Just so," the boy said. And Leal followed his master out into Ivlin, City of the Light, talking the whole way.

I set my quill down with a sigh. It has taken me nearly a decade, but I have finished. The account of my friends' adventures in the mind world is finally complete. Stella, never far from my desk, twinkles her approval. I stare out the window at the crashing waves on the sand as I massage my aching neck. This is my favorite room in our new home. The tall windows let in plenty of light so that I hardly ever have need of a candle while I work. And the steady pounding of the waves calms my mind when it begins to wander from the task at hand, though the view is often more of a distraction than an aid. I don't believe I will ever quite get used to the spectacular beauty of a coastal sunset.

"Mother!" My own young Leal comes barreling into

the room. "Mother, it's nearly time for the festival to start! Aren't you ready yet? Uncle Gil and Aunt Ashlyn are here to collect us."

It seems I've lost track of the time again. Not that it surprises anyone. "I'm sorry, Leal. Let me just fix my hair and I'll be right out." Turning, I get a good look at my eager boy of seven. He must have been sneaking around with Gil's eldest again, as he's managed to get dirt smeared all over his face. "You are not quite ready yet either, my child. Go wash up and put on clean trousers." He groans but runs to do my bidding.

Groaning in my turn, I rise from the chair with difficulty. It is becoming a more difficult task every day as the child within me grows. I shuffle my way to the mirror in my room and quickly brush my hair out. I've just finished when the pounding of small feet alerts me to my son's reappearance.

"I'm all clean now!"

"Let me see." I make a show of looking him over. He is, in fact, far cleaner than I often manage to get him, though traces of dirt can still be seen along his chin. "Well, I suppose you'll have to do." I sigh. "Where's your Aunt Ami?"

"She was here a while back but didn't want to disturb you. She said that she must go ahead to help with the preparations. Please, can't we go now?"

"In a few minutes, you little whirlwind." Eamon chuckles as he enters the room. "Now, help Uncle Gil hitch the horses. You know your mother mustn't walk long distances in her present condition."

"Yes, Father." The boy bounces out of the room as quickly as he came.

Eamon's face clouds the moment Leal has left. He crosses the room and leans close. "I don't mean to worry you, but Ackley has just arrived. He asked to speak with you, and I left him in the kitchen to wait."

My brow furrows. "Uncle is here? Why now?" I have had no word from him in years. And though we moved to Ivlin shortly after our marriage, our location has not been a secret. I have long prepared for this day. I press a hand to my expanding stomach and take a deep breath. I have children to think of now.

Eamon lifts my chin, so our eyes meet. "I don't think he means any harm. Still, it's your choice, Giselle. You don't have to see him if you don't want to."

"No, he's come a long way." I sigh. "It wouldn't be right to put him out without speaking first."

"Very well. I'll be right beside you the whole time."

Eamon keeps his hand at my back as we enter the kitchen. I stop short just inside the door, half in shock. I have never seen Uncle look so good. The previously unkempt beard has been neatly trimmed. The ill-fitting coat replaced with a finely tailored one. And most importantly, the bloodshot eyes are now unclouded and strong.

He clears his throat when he sees me. "Hello,

Giselle." Even the acidic voice has mellowed, though it still holds a gruff edge.

"Uncle, welcome."

He twists his hat in his hands. "I...I didn't mean to intrude. I just..." He clears his throat again, shifting his feet. "Was that your boy I saw at the pump?"

I stiffen and Eamon wraps his arm around my shoulders. "Yes," I reply with more force than I intended.

"Ah, very good. Fine lad, fine lad." He gestures to me. "And you're looking well."

"Yes, thank you." I relax and smile slightly. "So are you, Uncle."

"I've been working hard. To quit the drink, I mean." There is a small note of pride in his voice.

I nod. "That's good, Uncle. I'm glad."

"I didn't want to see you again until I could say that." He draws himself up straight, looking me directly in the eye. "Giselle, I've come to ask your forgiveness."

With a laugh, all the tension drains out of me. "You had that a long time ago. I hold no grudge against you, Uncle. And I am truly happy to see you doing so well."

He begins fidgeting with his hat again. "Be that as it may, I owe you an explanation...for the curse. You see—"

"It's all right," I cut him off, "I can guess what you will say, and I understand. You were grieving, probably drunk, and terrified of losing me. So you called on the man who aided you once before. I'd wager you didn't truly understand what was happening."

He nods, solemnly. "By the time I realized, it was too late. I couldn't undo it. And so you became a constant reminder of the worthless man I was. I'm ashamed to say, I did not handle it well. You deserved so much better than me, my girl. I'm glad you've found it."

I nod, wrapping my arm tighter around Eamon. "Nothing will excuse your past actions, but I know you can grow to be better. I understand, Uncle, and I do forgive you."

He smiles for the first time I can remember. "Thank you, child. Now, I'll not trouble you any longer." He turns to go.

"Wait, Uncle!"

He pauses on the threshold, much as I once did.

"We celebrate Light's Return tonight, in thanksgiving to the Creative One for seeing us through the bleak months. Would you like to join us?"

He nods, and I think there are tears in his eyes. "Aye, I would like that very much."

I hold out my hand to him. "Then come. Meet the rest of your family."

As Uncle escorts me to the carriage, I hear my trusted friend.

Well done, dear heart! You have come far indeed and shall bring others further still. Never fear the hard road, for you are mine, and I am with you.

THE END

ACKNOWLEDGMENTS

I had no idea what I was getting myself into when I began this book! It has been quite the learning process, and so many wonderful people have helped me along the way. So, before I start giving shoutouts, I just want to say a great big thanks to everyone who has encouraged and supported me on this journey. You are all awesome and I appreciate you so very much!

But, since names must be given, I'll start with Professor Bishop. Without your Monster Essay this book would have never come to be. Thank you for creating such an engaging assignment to spark our creativity.

To my Drossburners and Betas: Your advice and encouragement has been invaluable. It's your words that have made *To Slay a Curse* what it is today. Thank you.

To my bestie and editor, Amanda: You somehow

managed to bathe my book baby in red ink without damaging my confidence. Quite the feat, my dear. Thank you for all the hard work.

To my talented friend LoriAnn: A major thanks for my gorgeous cover. It's such a perfect representation of this heart story of mine and I couldn't be more in love.

To my formatter, Elisabeth: You seriously saved my sanity. Thank you for all the lovely little touches that make these contents just as beautiful as their wrapping.

To my amazing Sisterhood: Thank you so much for your hard work getting the word out as I made this daunting leap into the realm of authorhood. Your excitement and encouragement have meant the world to me.

And above all, I give thanks to God. Without the talents you have gifted me and the love you have given me I would be no writer today. Thank you for showing me my worth and allowing me the opportunity to create with you.

ABOUT THE AUTHOR

A PROUD Hufflepuff and hard-core Tolkienite, Rae weaves fantastical tales filled with heart and hope for the YA reader. If you can catch her without her nose in a book or a pen in hand, she would be more than thrilled to share in an adventure or relax with a chai and chat. After growing up in several countries across Asia, she is now happily settled on the banks of the great Mississippi with her family.

This is her debut novel.

FIND RAE ONLINE

https://writerraegraham.com/

facebook.com/writerraegraham
twitter.com/writerraegraham
instagram.com/writerraesbooknook
goodreads.com/RaeGraham

www.ingramcontent.com/pod-product-compliance
Lightning Source LLC
Chambersburg PA
CBHW071548110726
47908CB00007B/2034